KEYS TO AN EMPTY HOUSE

KEYS TO AN EMPTY HOUSE

David Finkle

PLUM BAY PUBLISHING, LLC

Copyright © 2022 by David Finkle

All rights reserved. no part of this publication may be reproduced, distributed, or transmitted in any form or by any means, including photocopying, recording, or other electronic or mechanical methods, without the prior written permission of the publisher except in the case of brief quotations embodied in critical reviews and certain other noncommercial uses permitted by copyright law.

For permission requests, contact the publisher at the website below
Plum Bay Publishing, LLC
www.plumbaypublishing.com

Library of Congress Control Number: 2021920314
ISBN paperback: 978-1-7348848-3-8
ISBN ebook: 978-1-7348848-4-5

Printed in the United States of America
Cover design by Sonya Dalton
Interior layout by Barbara Aronica-Buck
Copyedited by Sally Fay

For Martin, Julia, Steve and, certainly, June

I can tell why a snail has a house.
—"King Lear," William Shakespeare

A chair is not a house.
—Lyric, "A House Is Not a Home," Hal David

i.

He is having trouble with the key. It is not engaging properly. It sticks. He jiggles it in the lock. He tries withdrawing it a fraction of an inch. He tries turning it again. Is he turning it in the right direction? In neither direction does the lock give. "Come on," he says to the lock and to himself. Nothing doing. "Come on," he says aloud. His unmodulated tone does not help. The pitch of his voice is never satisfying to him. It never has been, something about the lack of grounding timbre. He tries pushing the key farther in. He tries turning it again. Still no go. He withdraws it and takes it from his left hand. He is left-handed. He shakes his left hand, retrieves the key from his right. He tries again. He figures he will eventually get the hang of it. In his lengthy experience with houses and keys to them, this is almost always the case. Maybe the key he's using isn't the one to the parlor floor. Maybe it's meant for the below-stoop gate. No. When he picked the keys up from Mrs. Landau, the professionally clipped real estate agent expressly said—along with other cursory instructions about the house—that this was the main entrance key, the parlor-floor entrance. This green door. This forest-green door. She separated the key from the other four. It has a crudely cut square of cloth tape pressed on it that says "front door" in hand-written ink now blurred from possibly being used many times in the rain.

Ah, there it goes. It's engaging. It's turning. Finally. The forest-green door with its brass lion's-head knocker opens. He notes that the door needs a coat of paint, but he approves of the color. For a reason he has never understood, he has always preferred a green door, a forest-green door. He suspects it's a superstition he has had since childhood, or perhaps it has to do with, was it a popular song called "The Green Door"? Did the lyric to the song contain the words "hospitality's thin there"? He isn't certain. He suspects hospitality will be in short supply while he's in residence. He also suspects he will ask to have the shade of forest-green duplicated as closely as possible when any work he decides on is done to the door. That is, should he decide on having any work done at all. He may not be here long enough to make it worthwhile. He picks up the valise he brought with him. Everything else of importance he still owns and is to be with him in this latest—surely temporary, if the past is prologue, as it usually is for him—home will be delivered in the next few hours. That's what he has been promised. There isn't much. Once there was, much more. Much more. No longer.

He enters. He's inside. He shuts the forest-green door behind him. The brass lion's-head knocker makes a muted clunk. He had the urge to try it when he climbed the stoop. He did not act on the impulse. He would never need to use it. He holds the supreme hope that few others will. He did not count the steps. Had he done that, he would have had the number in his head every time he mounted them. He did not want that cluttering his mind. He is in the front hall. It's empty. It would be, wouldn't it? He inhales the musty smell houses empty for periods of time acquire. He's smelled it before. He knows it will disappear but has never decided whether it truly disappears or whether he just becomes accustomed to it.

He sets the valise down. The door to the living room is to his right. He walks through it. The living room, too, is empty. Almost empty. He didn't mind the emptiness. He prefers that to living in a furnished house. He does not want to feel as if he's settling into someone else's home. He has the money to cover whatever he needs. A carved-back Victorian chair does sit before one of the two high windows facing the street. The lace curtains hanging from rods above the windows and below the moldings that travel around the walls are pulled back. This allows the weak November sun to fall through the windows onto the chair. The sun may have fallen on it steadfastly, unforgivingly over the years. He undoes the tired velvet cords holding the curtains back. He wants them obscuring the room. Not to keep the sun out. To keep prying eyes from peering in as well as to shelter him from distracting activity on the street.

On the chair's backrest its upholstery depicts an embroidered eighteenth-century pastoral scene: a shepherd and a milkmaid shyly making eyes at each other. Like the curtains' cords, it's faded. Perhaps it should be reupholstered. Perhaps that's why the previous owners had abandoned it. Maybe it has to do with Mrs. Landau's mentioning that people don't want brown furniture anymore. What's wrong with brown furniture? What's wrong with people?

Mrs. Landau said the previous renters had left a few items behind. They are welcome to them, she said they had said of the subsequent tenant or tenants. He could do what he would with them. He looks at the chair. He touches the top of its intricately carved wooden frame. He moves the chair a few inches for no reason. He repositions it between the windows. Before people sit, this is what they often do without thinking: reposition what they're about to sit on. He sits. The chair creaks slightly. How old is it? He looks down and thinks he sees dust puff out from it. It's comfortable enough. He decides to keep it. For the time being. He gets up. He may never sit on it again. Maybe he will.

He turns his attention to the dining room through the open doors separating it from the living room. It is completely empty. He sees the marble fireplace on the east wall matching the marble fireplace in the living room, in what is called, more properly for the period in which the three-story house was built, the parlor. He prefers the English spelling: parlour. It seems more fitting for the designated space. For that matter, he prefers the English spelling of "humour," too. At the far end of the dining room, he sees an oriel window above a glass door leading to the garden. He walks towards it. He looks through it at a platform and some steps with a metal railing. A wrought-iron bench is at the bottom of the garden. It faces him. He thinks it has been placed that way so anyone sitting on it can see into the house and may be able to see anyone moving around inside. There are leaves on the bench. This November is a particularly drab November. The entire garden is covered with dried brown leaves, a large leaf duvet. He catches himself thinking the "duvet" bit and quickly dismisses the ludicrous poetic metaphor. No one has bothered to collect the leaves. No one would have. Mrs. Landau told him the house has been unoccupied for over a year. He had not thought to ask if she had any idea why. That would have suggested he had more interest in the history of the house than he had. It is a house like any other house. To complete the transaction, he was content to have as little conversation with Mrs. Landau as needed. Presumably, the leaves have fallen from the one tree in the garden. Perhaps some have been blown in from the trees he can see in neighboring gardens. All his life he has left botany to others. He has never mastered trees. He thinks these trees may be oaks. He has never been able to tell an oak from an elm from a maple from a sycamore from an ash. He does recognize a birch. A palm tree is no challenge. Neither is a weeping willow. He notices the outlines of flowerbeds. Nothing is growing in them now. There wouldn't be at this time of year. Possibly a late-blooming rose. He sees none. High wooden walls define the garden. Against the west wall he sees an espalier on which roses may have grown and could grow again. On it now he sees what appear to be dried stalks or vines. He wonders if anything will grow in the garden when spring comes. Something might, were he to see to it. Maybe he will. Maybe he will ask around about a gardener. Maybe Mrs. Landau will have a name. Maybe there will be some perennials about which he won't have to do anything. He will find out in the spring. If he is still here in the spring. Only time will tell. Let it. He has as little truck with time as he is able.

He leaves the room for the hall and the pervading smell of, the prevailing, pervasive smell of, emptiness. He looks at the staircases. There is the one leading downstairs where the below-stairs kitchen is at the front with the storage room at the back and the stone steps that lead to the garden. Metal doors cover that entrance to the garden. He assumes the doors are secured with a lock. One of the other four keys he has must be for that lock.

He stands in the hall. There's the staircase leading to the second story and to two bedrooms and the bathroom. He isn't certain whether he wants to go upstairs first or downstairs. He imagines the spaces. He has seen them. Mrs. Landau said they could be viewed online. Once he had done that, she offered to meet him at the house. He said he would just as soon not.

Visiting a succession of buildings did not appeal to him. Visiting even one didn't appeal to him. Walking through houses, making real estate small talk he regarded as tedious. He had seen and lived in a sufficient number of houses to understand that if he had ever been the house-proud type, he no longer was. He just wanted to live someplace undemanding. He just wanted to live somewhere where he would not be bothered. When he had seen the 73 East Ninth Street video in which a camera pans slowly around the rooms as if to an English-sounding air with an adagio indication—this, right after allowing a view of the façade with its reassuring (for him) forest-green door—he told Mrs. Landau, whom he had not yet met, that he would take it. He would take it at the actually reasonable rental specified. He would take it, although it was obvious to him nothing had been done with it to enhance its basic appearance. He had no interest in haggling. He had no need to. He could hear surprise in her voice. He could hear she was pleased. She was thinking of whatever commission she was about to earn for very little effort. He had heard similar responses from brokers with whom he had had dealings in the cities where he had previously lived, usually for short periods of time. He heard in her voice—he had no mental image of her—a tone that signaled she had decided she was conversing with someone who knew little about renting a home and perhaps wasn't worthy of this one. She might have suggested to him a different house, one she was having more trouble getting off her hands. That's if there was such a property. He could all but hear her decide it was too late for any manipulation.

Mrs. Landau put the paperwork in motion so that when he came to the office just off Washington Square—where she, a short, bulky, well-dressed woman, fussily presided over three younger women—he had only to sign on a few undotted lines. He had only to write a few checks. He had only to take the five keys. She handed them to him with a professional smile. They were attached to a string and a creased tag with the address on it. Mrs. Landau and he shook hands. She reprised her professional smile. That was that.

And now he is standing in the hall. He will go upstairs to the second-story bedrooms. He sees them in his mind's eye. The larger one is in back, the smaller one in front. The bathroom, which, according to Mrs. Landau, has been somewhat modernized, is directly in front of the staircase.

He climbs the stairs. As he does, he wonders how many times he will climb these stairs, how many times he will descend them in an hour, in a day, in a month, in the entire time he continues to live here. One of the stairs creaks. Another creaks. He wonders whether he will come to be annoyed with the creaks or whether he will come to be used to them, reassured by them. Will the times he is annoyed be equal to the times he is reassured?

He is at the top of the staircase. He notices how smooth and aligned the floorboards are. He knows they are old, perhaps the original floorboards, and have been carefully maintained over the years. By whom? By how many whoms? He peeks into the bathroom. He sees the bathtub on its claw-and-ball legs. He recognizes that it is a reproduction of a classic bathtub. He sees the obviously latterly introduced showerhead, the toilet, the small window at the far end with its pebbled, opaque lower pane. He sees the wash basin. It is also designed to conjure an earlier, perhaps more elegant, era. The mirrored door on the cabinet above it is slightly ajar. He sees part of himself reflected in it. His reflection is not something he cares to linger on. He knows his aging face, his slackening body well enough.

He leaves the bathroom to examine the bedrooms. They are empty, but for the fireplaces in both with mirrors over them that need resilvering. He thinks of skin diseases that might have been rampant in the Middle Ages. The proportions of the rooms are satisfactory. So is the closet space. The closets will accommodate the little he needs to place in them. There was a time when he had many suits he might have hung there. Now he has three he hardly ever wears. They are in the four trunks that will arrive later. He thinks of the Henry David Thoreau quote that goes, "Beware of all enterprises that require new clothes." He goes Thoreau one better. He is wary of all enterprises for which old clothes would suffice. These days and for some time he is wary of all enterprises that involve others. Full stop.

What he does not decide is which of the bedrooms he will make his. He has no intention of settling on one and designating the other a guest room. If he puts a bed in both, he can decide from night to night and on the spur of the moment in which he will sleep. He only has one bed arriving today. He will have the movers put it in the back bedroom. That room will be quieter. It overlooks the garden. Thanks to his last house, the one set back from Hoyt Lane in Bedford, he is again used to hearing no street noise. He liked living there until he no longer liked living there. He bought it because he missed the country. He sold it because he missed the city. He recognizes there is a pattern to his moves. He has no inclination to analyze the pattern. He has no inclination to attempt to change it. He has no inclination to do anything about it one way or another. Other than running a piece of doggerel quoted at him by his Uncle Moe when he was a child. The one that included the lines, or lines like it, "When it's hot he wants it cold/When it's cold he wants it hot." He doesn't recall its origin. He knows it is not the nursery rhyme that begins, "Pease porridge hot." But that's who he is, all right: someone who when it's cold likes it hot, and vice versa. He has always been that way. No reason to change himself now, is there? Is he even capable of change? He doubts it.

He returns to the hallway and to the staircase reaching the third floor. He climbs it. None of the stairs creak. Is that due to its being traveled less often? He enters what he already knows to be a single large room lined in part with low shelves—shelves good for books—and interrupted by the expected fireplaces. He could not tell from Mrs. Landau's video whether the room had been more than one room at an earlier time. He couldn't tell for what it, or they, had been used. He thinks a child's bedroom or more than one child's bedroom must have been there at some time. Perhaps it had been a single child's bedroom and a playroom or, given the shelves, a library next to a bedroom not necessarily for a child. Over the years it might have been used for several purposes. Likely, it has been.

He can use the entire space as a library, as a study. He does have books. That's one item he has plenty of, for obvious reasons. Yes, the large third-story room will be his library. There will be no pool table in it. He is not transporting the pool table he left behind in the Bedford house, the one that had been left behind by the previous occupants and perhaps by occupants before that. This will be the library-study. It will be only the library-study because at the far end is a commodious club chair now facing the window overlooking the garden, which he had already decided he would enjoy. As much as he enjoys anything, that is. He will at least not be averse to overlooking the gardens and the backs of a row of houses on East Tenth Street. He recalls that in Alfred Hitchcock's *Rear Window* the house in which the James Stewart character lives is on the south side of West Ninth Street, looking through to Eighth Street. He contents himself, as much as he is ever able to content himself, that he will not experience anything even vaguely comparable to what Stewart's character experienced. The last thing on his mind is giving time over to observing neighbors surreptitiously. He hasn't the slightest interest in neighbors, whoever they might be. He is most interested in their manifesting no interest in him.

He goes to the club chair. It is covered in an olive-green fabric that, like the chair in the living room, has seen better, brighter days. He thinks, *I* have seen better, brighter days, but how long ago was that? He sits. He's as comfortable as he has been in a while. I am home, he thinks. He thinks, I am as at home as I ever expect to be in this life. For the time being, this will be his library-study, and this is where he will sit. He will put his books on these shelves. On these shelves he will arrange—in no particular order—the books he's kept after paring down their once vast number. He will take them down to read. Some—the vast majority—he will take down to reread.

For the time being, anyway. He thinks the at-home feeling he's experiencing will pass. He knows it will pass. It has before. Has it ever! Indeed, it already has passed. It has passed, as it does whenever he arrives at his latest—well, "squat" is as good a word as any—at his latest squat. He relaxes—if "relaxes" is appropriate for the recurring moment—into the familiar reverie, into his familiar reverie. He has no control over that. He knows he has no control over that. It just happens. It forces itself on him. It intrudes. This reverie could be called taking stock. Every time, dammit, no matter where he has just established himself yet again, he takes stock of where he is, of where he has been, of where he might be next.

By now there have been so many nexts. There have been so many nexts when he thought he would figure out, when, if he were lucky, he would determine, what he wants of life. There have been so many nexts when he wondered if he honestly wanted anything of life, anything at all. There have been so many nexts when he occasionally wondered if he had anything to contribute to life. Contribute to life? Contributing to life—there's a self-aggrandizing conceit, if ever there was one.

He never got lucky on any of it. He never reached any conclusions. Not true. He always reached the same conclusion. That's "conclusion" in the singular: He won't spend any time thinking about his life. As much as is possible, he will try not to spend any time thinking about anything. Instead, he will read here—and read only in part as an escape from drawing conclusions about that great thing called life, that great overrated thing called life. Instead, he may even write here. Perhaps. Perhaps not. That remains to be seen. "It's unlikely," he says aloud to himself. Truth is, he never expects to write again.

ii.

For this new 73 East Ninth Street, New York City resident is Elihu Goulding. The name is known. At one time in the increasingly retreating past, it was even well known. It's definitely known by people of a certain age who are readers. Even people who are not of a certain age, people who are not readers may hear a far-away bell ringing. He is Elihu Goulding the author. He is the same Elihu Goulding who, at twenty-six, published *Wandering Youth*. He is the same Elihu Goulding who, at twenty-nine, published *For My Betters*. He is the Elihu Goulding who was reviewed extremely favorably on the cover of *The New York Times Book Review* by Alfred Kazin for *Wandering Youth*. He is the author who was reviewed extremely favorably on the cover of *The New York Times Book Review* by Elizabeth Hardwick for *For My Betters*. He is the Elihu Goulding whose *Wandering Youth* was on *The New York Times* and *Publishers Weekly* bestseller lists, respectively, one hundred four weeks and one hundred six weeks. He is the Elihu Goulding who was on the cover of *Time* in a David Levine caricature when *For My Betters* was published and that week alone sold upwards of fifty thousand copies. He has the Levine caricature framed. Somewhere. He does not know where. It will turn up. Or it won't. He is the Elihu Goulding who received the Pulitzer Prize for his first novel and the National Book Award for his second. He is the Elihu Goulding who, on the basis of *Wandering Youth* and *For My Betters*, received the Douglas F. Scargill Award in Literature from the American Academy of Arts and Letters. He is the Elihu Goulding who sold the movie rights to *Wandering Youth* for one million two hundred thousand dollars and the

For My Betters movie rights for two million five hundred thousand dollars and then joked with Johnny Carson on *The Tonight Show* about both sales. He is the Elihu Goulding from whom Johnny Carson kiddingly asked for a loan, calling him by his then, now no longer used, nickname "Eli." (Who was around to use it?) It was a joke that had Ed McMahon cracking up. The footage of it appeared for at least ten years on anniversary shows devoted to excerpts from the comedian-host's funniest moments. Elihu believes the footage had not been included on those shows much after that. He has no interest in checking, and no one ever mentioned it to him during the time Carson stayed on the air, not that he has ever spoken to many people who might have brought it up. He was never invited to chat with Jay Leno for reasons that need no explanation to those who know Elihu Goulding's story. As compared to his stories. Whether he is known to Jimmy Kimmel or to Jimmy Fallon or to Stephen Colbert or to James Corden or to Seth Meyers remains undisclosed. The likely short answer is: No, he is not known to them.

Nowadays he is the Elihu Goulding who recoils from running his credits, his accomplishments, his early successes. Even to himself. More than anything, to himself. He wants nothing to do with them, though he can never divorce himself from them. For better or worse, they are part of him. Mostly for worse, as he sees it. But he can hope. He can hope that days, if not weeks, will go by without his having to consider those supposed accomplishments, without his having to confront them. Occasionally, he gets lucky, and that happens. He fails to think about them for a day, maybe two. Then there he is, thinking again.

The restlessness never ends. It wanes but never completely abates. When he was writing *Wandering Youth*, he could not have known that the unnamed discontent that lay behind its writing is a lifelong manifestation, a lifelong affliction. If he had sensed it would be, he might never have written the damned tome to begin with, or, come to that, *For My Betters*. He had not sensed it. If anything, he thought the writing of them was therapeutic. He hoped it would be. He was twenty-two when he began to write the first novel. He was in his senior year at Yale. He wrote the first chapter as his final assignment for the class in creative writing taught by Robert Penn Warren. He received an A for the paper, i.e., for the chapter. Alongside the A, scratched with a pen and not a ballpoint, three-time Pulitzer Prize winner Penn Warren had written, "Very good. I encourage you to think about expanding this."

He had already been thinking about expanding it. The encouragement was all he needed to add chapters before and after the chapter he had called "The Kissing Bandit." The A-worthy chapter was about a boy and girl on a prom date and the awkward advances towards their goodnight kiss when both of them had had previous sexual experiences. The chapter was fictionalized autobiography. Of course it was. *Wandering Youth* was almost entirely fictionalized autobiography. So was *For My Betters*. In his many interviews and on his many book tours, he denied that either was. He did acknowledge parsimoniously that no first novelist would be likely not to include details from his past. "What young writer wouldn't do the same?" he repeatedly asked interviewers giving him unconvinced looks. Over and again during question-and-answer exchanges at the end of readings across the country, in England and even in Paris at The Village Voice bookstore on Rue Princesse, he said that if his book had succeeded, it was due to its reflecting the histories of his generation. He reiterated that the "*Youth*" of the title referred not to an individual but to an aggregate as observed by an individual. He insisted he was not that individual. He insisted he was using "youth" in the plural but that the title *Wandering Youths* was klutzy. He insisted that although much of the novel was set in Trenton, New Jersey, where he was born, he was writing about young men everywhere. He insisted he was using a particular to represent a universal. He maintained that although he was born in 1950, as was his protagonist Seth Levy, any similarity was coincidental.

Of other admissions of similarities between Seth, *For My Betters* protagonist Sabe Levensohn, and him was the three of them as only children. Okay, all right, he'd say when pressed on his experiences as an only child and his evidently convincing portraits of Seth and Sabe as such were due to his own past. He never brought up in later interviews, however, an undeniable fact he was able to deny by offering no one the opportunity to ask about it in the first place. He did not want to deal with this undeniable fact for the hardly simply reason that he might not have been an only child.

The truth was/is that Elihu could have come into the world as a second son, a circumstance about which he was unaware at the time he wrote *Wandering Youth* and *For My Betters*. He did not know—he had no way of knowing, neither his mother Jean nor his father Morris had ever told him—that two years before he arrived, Jean had had a miscarriage. She'd lost a boy, a boy whom they were going to call Elihu. It was an event so understandably sorrowful that Jean and Morris decided they would never talk of it.

Least of all to Elihu, who learned about it only after he'd published his first two books and then not from Jean or Morris. The beans were spilled—if as offhand an expression as that one is permissible—by his Aunt Essie, his father's sister, who was always joked about in the family, if not outright denigrated as an exasperating gossip.

It came to pass this way: Shortly after *For My Betters* began climbing the charts, Essie and her husband Herb, often visibly embarrassed by Essie, were over for Friday dinner. Elihu was in Trenton for one of his fewer and fewer visits. Just as those gathered were finishing the main course—brisket with potatoes and carrots—a lull fell on the conversation. Essie, never comfortable with lulls, ended it with, "Oh, Eli, I've been meaning to ask you." Everyone turned to her. He noticed Essie had taken on the look of fake sincerity he'd come to recognize as one of her favorite colloquial tactics. She said, "I've just read For Your Betters"—of course, she meant *For My Betters* but may have been thinking she was one of Elihu's betters—"and it's wonderful. Maybe not as good as *Wandering Youth* but right up there. And I noticed in both of them the main characters are only children. Since I know the books are about you and our family, I wondered why you didn't mention the miscarriage in either of the books."

Silence fell around the table like the shadow of an eclipse. Elihu said, "What miscarriage? What are you talking about?"

Essie answered, with disingenuousness thickening her voice, "Oh, you didn't know. You don't know." She looked around the table in manufactured horror. "Oh, I thought you did. I shouldn't have said anything"—all this spoken with the irrefutably implicit understanding that Essie absolutely knew he didn't know and that no, she shouldn't have said anything, since no one else had deliberately said anything for years.

Jean said nothing now. Morris quickly said, "Essie, Elihu, that's a conversation for another time. We're here for Elihu's newest success and just being happy he's able to be with us."

"We certainly are," Essie said, as if she were the long-agreed-upon designated family conciliator.

The rest of the dinner went on as if nothing had been said, yet with the unmistakable undercurrent that something of supreme importance had been said and now had to be ignored at whatever cost.

Jean and Morris were smart enough to know that the exchange couldn't be left unexplained. Once the others had left and Elihu, Jean and Morris were alone, Morris reintroduced the subject. They were all tidying up the dining-room table. Morris, who ran his accounting firm with his standard seriousness, said, "Elihu, about what Essie said. Before you were born, your mother had a miscarriage. We thought it was something you never needed to know about. Why would you? It would have little or no bearing on you." Jean said, "Why would you need to know?" Morris continued, "Don't think we were keeping it from you. It was only there was no reason for you to know. Now you do. Essie knew better than to say anything. But that's Essie. She'll never change." Jean said, "We were going to name him Elihu. That's why we were so happy when you were born. You were, you are, the Elihu we always wanted."

At that, the subject was dropped, never again to be brought up. At the time Elihu had considered mentioning it in the future if and when the time seemed right. Through the end of Jean's and Morris's lives the time never seemed right. He wasn't going to ask Essie. Nonetheless, from then on he thought he understood the faraway gaze Jean would let interrupt her usually good (cultivated?) humor every now and again for no more than a few seconds.

And since Elihu knew none of this previous to his first two novels, he assured himself it had no bearing on creating the fictional Seth Levy or Sabe Levensohn. Had he known, would he have? Would he have written about them as elder sons? He couldn't begin to speculate. From time to time, he did find it necessary to purge the cheap thought that in some way knowing about the previous Elihu would have somehow compromised, even invalidated *Wandering Youth* and *For My Betters*. He realized he ought not be relieved that he hadn't known, but he was. He had to admit there was shame in that, and for no substantive reason the shame compounded his attitude towards the cumbersome blockbusters.

Anyway, it was too late for getting around to the disorienting family secret in proliferating later *For My Betters* interviews. He set aside the update. Over time it barely crosses his mind. He doesn't regard himself as repressing or suppressing it. He's merely dropped it into a lower mind's drawer where he'd come upon it only when searching for something else from his less-retained past.

The larger point Elihu insisted on repeatedly making was that Seth Levy is a composite, that Sabe Levensohn, too, is a composite. He repeated the contention, as if it were a mantra. That was his story about his story, and he stuck to it.

But when he looks back now at the adamant denials then, he views them as foolishness, as rank silliness. He wonders what pretense he was trying to keep up. He thinks that whatever pretense it was backfired. He has reason to think now that he might have been better off had he not inserted his Trenton childhood and youth into that precocious *Bildungsroman*. He has reason to think now that he might have been better off had he never written the precocious *Bildungsroman*. Or its sequel. Had he not, he would have had a different life. He could not have failed to. He could not have had the life he had had right up to this minute. For the thousandth or millionth time, he thought that if he had not written *Wandering Youth* and compounded it with *For My Betters*, his life would have been something else absolutely, something inevitably improved.

Yet, he had written both books. There was no getting away from it, from them. There *is* no getting away from it or them. He sits in the olive-green club chair gazing out the window at the garden and above it the sky in which dark grey clouds are tumbling his way. He forces himself to understand, again, that there was a time when getting away from any of it was the last thing he wanted to do. He wanted to go with it. He wanted to wrap himself in it, revel in it, wallow in it, maximize it. He wanted to do anything he could to make it last forever. Making it last forever would not be difficult, he had reckoned. All he had to do was accept the invitations to visit not only Johnny Carson and *The Tonight Show* but to sit on couches next to Mike Douglas and Merv Griffin, to accept the requests to speak at Princeton, Harvard and alma mater Yale. He composed a tough-minded speech delivered when, at thirty-five, he received an honorary degree from Yale. He likened the class of 1985 to the wandering youth(s) of his bestseller and confided to them his inflexible conviction that "despite all, if dreams have to be persistently pursued in order to come true and *are* persistently pursued, they *will* come true." He said *his* dreams had. He sits in the olive-green club chair and thinks that if he were addressing next year's Yale graduating class, he would give a wholly different speech. He would debunk dreams and give hard reality pride of place. He would say that hard reality is all there is.

But this is now and that was then. Then, despite his beliefs about Ronald Reagan and the American economy, he accepted the invitation to sit on a Yale board considering the advancing aims of higher education. He accepted an additional three hundred thousand dollars to adapt *Wandering Youth* for the screen. He accepted his being replaced for the second draft as no more than the inevitable ways of Hollywood. He helped promote the movie on the talk shows that were still eager to have him back on their plush couches. He signed a development deal with Norman Lear for a comedy series about law students, despite his not knowing more about law students than anyone else did. He hobnobbed with Lear, Beatrice Arthur, Louise Lasser. He had it socked to him by Judy Carne on *Rowan & Martin's Laugh-In*. He got to know Lily Tomlin. *Wandering Youth* and *For My Betters* were translated into many languages. They were bestsellers in France, *For My Betters* compared by one French critic to Gustave Flaubert's *Sentimental Education*. *Sentimental Education* being one of his favorite novels, he lapped up the praise. When he promoted the volumes in Paris, speaking French not well but well enough for the French to appreciate his efforts, he actually sat with other guests on Bernard Pivot's *Apostrophes*. One of the other guests was Marguerite Duras. She invited him for lunch, where she candidly discussed, among other subjects, her opinions of Jean-Paul Sartre and Simone de Beauvoir. He understood most of what she said. He also had the feeling she was flirting with him but only out of satisfying what she assumed was his expectation that she flirted with any reasonably attractive young man she met. He was asked to join a group of writers on a post-war trip to Vietnam and Cambodia. Although he had opposed the war when he was in his teens, he regarded it as his duty to supply himself with more firsthand knowledge of what had transpired in Khe Sanh, in Phnom Penh, in the killing fields, et cetera, so that he could speak about the conflict more authoritatively. The trip was led by the journalist Frances Fitzgerald, whom he came to respect for her ability to discourse on the war in an historical context.

He found time to write, of course. He was Elihu Goulding. Writing was obligatory. He wanted to write a novel about turn-of-the-century immigration pegged to what he knew of his father's parents and his mother's parents. He did write it. He called it *The Accidental Immigrants*. It did not do well. It was not reviewed on the front cover of *The New York Times Book Review* but in a respectful, though not enthusiastic, inside notice. It was the occasion of a discourse in *The New York Review of Books* by a fellow novelist who questioned retrospectively the sustained literary worth of *Wandering Youth* and *For My Betters*. The essay, which he committed to memory in large part, while trying to dismiss it, closed with the sentences, "Having mined his past for two works about childhood, adolescence and early manhood, Goulding has looked elsewhere for content and not found sufficient substance. The inference is that he has exhausted his natural material and may have nowhere else to go. Let us hope that is not the case."

Yes, let us hope that is not the case, Elihu thought about the condescending kiss-off, although it appears to be the case and has been the case for some time. There has been no fourth novel. There has been no outline for a fourth novel. There has been only the most fleeting glimmers of plot, of elusive thoughts, that, if they even stayed in his head for more than a minute, he then dismissed.

Sitting in the club chair, his arms on the armrests as if he has sat there looking out the window for years, as if he has sat there gazing out the window for decades, he parses again what he has refused to categorize as writer's block. He is not blocked. He considers writer's block an unconscious condition when a writer claims he or, of course, she, wants to write. In his estimation, writer's block occurs when a writer sits facing a blank page in frustration, or these days when a writer faces a blank computer screen. But Elihu hasn't faced a blank page since he can't remember when. He has never faced a blank computer screen. He abandoned writing before he might have written on a computer. That is not what he's doing. It is not that he wants to write but something is holding him back. It is that he does *not* want to write. He *chooses* not to write. If he wanted, he is convinced he could remove the block he has put between himself and a fourth novel and then a fifth and so on.

He doesn't want to ruminate on this any longer—on what he wants or unwaveringly doesn't from this life. This house is new to him. These circumstances are new to him. For the moment he suspects that if he remains seated, he will continue to think about his writing, about his *not* writing. It isn't the first time he has realized that for him club chairs are critically conducive to self-reflection. It is not the first time Elihu (the once-upon-a-longer-and-longer-ago time Eli) has judged that in his case self-reflection is unprofitable. Not that he has been able to stop. Is anyone able to stop, he wonders, again not for the first or the millionth time.

He rises from the chair and, undecided about what he wants to look at next, returns to the front of the room rather than leave it by the door in the rear. He walks slowly. He takes each step more slowly than the preceding one until he is at a complete standstill. Standing there, something comes over him, something completely unbidden, something from somewhere in him he senses he cannot plumb, an urge for which he has no clue to origins.

Unable to stop himself—how do you stop a surging wave before it crashes?—he shouts, "Something is killing me, and I don't know what it is."

Instantly, he looks around to see if anyone has heard him. He is well aware that no one could have heard him, but all the same he is embarrassed and shocked. He shudders. Shuddering is not something he remembers ever doing before. Instantly, he acknowledges to himself that it doesn't matter whether anyone else has heard the first words he has spoken aloud in the house. In this empty house. *He* has heard them. Furthermore, he knows that, having emitted them so dramatically, he will now have to deal with them, with what he knows he must regard as unexplored anguish.

iii.

Something is killing me, and I don't know what it is. He *won't* deal with them, with it, as he stands surrounded by vacant space and silent walls, by the twin fireplaces with their gaping mouths. He won't, because somewhere deeper even than the place from which the cry emanated he *does* know what it is that's killing him. He's convinced that something is indeed killing him, and he doesn't want to face what it is. It's as simple as that.

What to do instead? Masturbate. That's the first thing he thinks to do. "To keep anxiety at bay," his analyst, Friedrich Kloss, had put it many years before. He has to laugh at that one, an unexpressed ironic laugh. Masturbation, jerking off, whacking off, beating his meat, pulling his pud, spanking the monkey, wanking—the adolescent's handy fallback. So typical. Predictable in a teenager but pointless in a man of a certain age, that age being sixty-three. He hasn't masturbated for so long he wonders if he even remembers how. Of course, he remembers how, although he hadn't gone too expansively into the practice for either *Wandering Youth* or *For My Betters*. Philip Roth had beat him to it, so to speak. Philip Roth had *not*, as far as he knew, recorded the pleasures of someone else stroking a man's erect member. He had mentioned that in *Wandering Youth* but had finally redlined it after concluding the passage was still too Philip Roth-y for him.

He stroked with his left hand when he was a habitual practitioner and, while at it, constructed elaborate fantasies. He no longer even traffics—under any circumstances—in fantasies elaborate or spare. He hasn't for eons. He forsook them when his commitment to reality kicked in. He regards his penis as no more than the appendage through which he empties his bladder. Nighttime erections he regards as a negligible biological episode to be waited out, or, better yet, as happening to someone else.

Empty his bladder: an activity in which he can indulge noncommittally. He leaves the room, goes down the stairs to the bathroom opposite the other staircase and urinates. While doing that, he notes, as he does every time he urinates, that his flow is no longer that of a young man. Rather than scrutinize his meandering stream or contemplate the effects of Flomax, pro or con, he sizes up the toilet bowl. It's porcelain and, despite the bathroom's having been updated, has many cracks in it. Why, he wonders, is there such a mix of old-fashioned and new-fangled fixtures in the house? Whose taste is reflected here, how many different tastes?

He reaches for the handle, flushes. The apparatus operates well enough. When he's lived in homes less than an easy drive for the local handymen, he learned how to fix plumbing, rewire lamps, that sort of household thing few of his friends (which friends, what friends?) have mastered.

He turns to catch himself again in the mirror over the porcelain sink. He's learned how to avoid seeing himself in mirrors. Even when he shaves, he sees only the part of his face he's ridding of whiskers, so much of his beard now grey. He almost never takes in his entire face. He knows his face as well as he wants to—the high creased brow, the eyes black as eight balls, the ruddy cheeks, the slightly hooked nose, the full lips, the cleft chin. It's what's left of a one-time amusing young novelist's face, once a face looking both lived-in and innocent. He knows his five-foot-ten-inch body well enough. He knows what's happened to his pectorals, he's accustomed to the roll at his waist, he's seen his chest and pubic hair begin to grey, he knows the varicose veins prominent in both legs—an inheritance from both his parents, and, he assumes, from their parents before them.

Fuck knowing his face or torso any better. He zips his fly as he goes to leave the bathroom and says, again aloud but in a muted tone, "Za." He hears himself say it and thinks, "Za." I haven't said that in years. I haven't thought it.

Now he thinks of Anne Marie, about whom he also hasn't thought in years. Anne Marie Goodson with whom he had had a marvelous affair thirty years before. It lasted until she'd been diagnosed with ovarian cancer and decided what she must do was to fight it at the Brownsville, Texas, home where her parents still lived. She went there to die with, as she phrased it, "peace and pizzazz."

It was Anne Marie, built like a blond spark plug and fitted with a spark plug's energy, who introduced the nonsense syllable "Za" to him. As far as he knew, she had coined it for declaring in any number of situations, an utterance applicable for all occasions. Actually, she invoked it most frequently to suggest that everything was as it was, as it appeared for good or ill, for better or worse. A short way of saying, So be it.

Why had it come to him then? It was himself acknowledging *to* himself that he was now at his new East Ninth Street address for good or ill, for better or worse. He hopes for good, for better. Maybe not for ill, not for worse. He questions the meager hope. Now he imagines it will be for neither better *nor* worse. It hadn't been for better or worse at any of his several previous addresses. For better: That's what he wants. He doesn't know what he wants.

"So be it" imposes itself on him, hinting that wherever he is, whatever he's experiencing, that might already signal the beginning of something worse, something maybe even volcanic building up in him.

He doesn't repeat "Za," but he hears himself think it. Standing at the top of the stairs, he thinks, I know what I need. I need music. I need music to drown out the echoes in my head. I rarely think about music, but I'm thinking about music now. Now I am thinking about it. Classical music. Haydn, Handel. Not Mozart, not Telemann, not Vivaldi. He hankers for a stateliness that will ground him, something evocative of imposed order—order he hasn't been able to impose on himself.

Handel's *Concerti Grossi*. That would do it. It would do something. He hasn't thought of them in years. They weren't really his thoughts then, either. They were someone else's. Whose? Who had introduced them to him? Which man of his acquaintance? Which woman? Yes, it was a woman, whose eyes went blurry when she listened to them. She would come to him. When she did, he would recognize that it was not so much the music that engulfed him. It was her reaction to the music.

He knew the term "I was lost in the music." Who used it? Who used it, despite his never quite understanding what she meant? He understood the words, but the concept escaped him. It implied to him her somehow unguardedly entering the music, helplessly pulled into an alien landscape until the music ended and she was released through no action of her own. But what explains experiencing that feeling? He never had.

Now that he thinks about it, now that the idea of getting lost in a foreign clime made of carefully contrived notes has suddenly taken him over, notes that inexorably draw him into them, he understands something, perhaps understands something about whoever it was impressed them on him. Or he doesn't understand but at least unexpectedly shares something with the (temporarily?) forgotten person with whom he never had shared, never had found a way to share when it counted.

One thing he suspects about her, and about him in regard to her, is that it could have been his give-or-take attitude towards music that had eventually come between them. He has the thought, ironic now, that if he had hit on the Handel hankering he's now having out of nowhere, out of something the origins of which he can't trace—who was it? who *was* it?—if he'd had it even once with her and had said so, that would have been enough to smooth over their differences, their growing differences. Having had it now, could he contact her on, say, the pretext of borrowing 78s, 33s, cassettes, CDs and thereby revive the relationship? But no, he can't contact whoever she is about this. She would suspect something was up and would not want it. If he denied an ulterior motive, she wouldn't believe him. Whoever she was. It's on the tip of his memory.

Despite there being no ulterior motive of any stripe, he has no intentions of reviving anything. Whoever she is, she's like former lovers in the lives of so many people. He cannot recall why he was in love with this her, or with any of the dismissed hers, what it felt like to be in love with any of them, or even if he ever was. More likely, he was not.

At the moment he just wants to listen to Handel. He has a sudden and necessary craving for Handel. Pure and simple.

iv.

As money is no object for him, he splurges on a sound system for the entire house. He installs it himself. The hammering and hanging give him something mindless to do for a few hours. He might have had the delivery men take care of that for a hefty tip. He has no financial worries. He has always husbanded his finances wisely, aided by advisors—his lawyers, his accountant—with whom he keeps in contact. From a distance.

The sound system is the first thing he does, even as the few pieces of furniture arrive that he sometimes moves into wherever he's decided to inhabit for the time being and sometimes, when he's taken a furnished place, puts into storage. There's the (undesirable?) brown four-poster bed and dining-room table that meant so much to his mother, Jean, and about which his father, Morris, never said anything, always having made a show of leaving household furnishings to his wife as her province. There is his dad's desk with the tooled inlaid center which he thought would be where he wrote when he inherited it but which came to him after he had ceased writing. He regards it now solely for sentimental value, as the tangible memory of where his physician father scribbled prescriptions in a hand only a pharmacist could read. To Elihu, the desk will always remain the place where his father read every *Journal of the American Medical Association* issue cover to cover. The acronym "JAMA" hews to Elihu's brain as if printed on a billboard in large capital letters.

There are the two convertible couches he installs in the upstairs library-study, one towards the front, one towards the back. Though he purchases many-threaded sheets, a comforter and pillows to supply the four-poster, he sleeps four nights out of five on one or the other of the convertible beds in their unconverted state. Sometimes he unwittingly falls asleep over a book in the club chair by which he positions a gooseneck lamp found in a Bowery outlet. He slumbers in various states of dress, sometimes fully clothed in whatever he woke up wearing that morning, sometimes just in boxers. Who's to know? When the housekeeper he's employed, a normally expressionless Mrs. Woolard, rings on Thursday mornings, he has enough time to throw on a shirt and pull on trousers before shuffling downstairs to let her in and then disappear to any of the rooms she's not tidying at the moment. He usually remembers to silence the Handel. Not always. He has to admit he doesn't care one way or the other what Mrs. Woolard, for whom he has made a spare set of keys but hasn't yet given her, thinks as she goes about her business throughout a house where various *Concerti Grossi* recordings are regularly piped into every room.

The chair his father had at the desk—upholstered in green leather and with the armrests faded from the weight of his father's arms—also made the furniture cut, along with the dining-room table, the leaves for which have gone missing years earlier. Had he been a man prone to arranging large or even relatively small dinner parties, he might have been perturbed, but he isn't, not as he would have been in his gregarious thirties. He thinks back on those times and wonders who that sociable Eli Goulding was, who that magnanimous fellow was cavalierly snatching the bill at quickly arranged dinners for eight or ten. Who were those spur-of-the-moment eight or ten? He barely recalls. Others probably included fellow novelists, male and female, for whom he was showing off.

More of his mother's belongings placed in the downstairs kitchen cabinets and kitchen drawers are the Lenox chinaware for twelve and the sterling silver for as many. Patterns the names of which are unknown to him, though one day, if he remembers, he will turn a dinner plate over to see what it says. He must have known at one time, since he's certain he included the information in the, yes, autobiographical *Wandering Youth*. He has never reread it to find out. He long since has made a commitment to himself never to reread either *Wandering Youth* or *For My Betters* and certainly not *The Accidental Immigrants*.

Again, he wonders who the man was who thought he might always openly invite as many as eleven others to eat from his inherited plates and with his inherited (pattern also unknown) silverware. He places the cookbooks he saved on a kitchen counter between bookends that boast tiny caryatids, bookends he cannot remember having purchased. Had Jean? He has her much-used cookbooks not because he assumes he would ever cook anything more complicated than scrambled eggs but because every once in a long while he thinks perhaps he *might* cook something more complicated than scrambled eggs. Jean had taught him the simpler things at a stove or oven. Occasionally, he still uses what he'd learned.

Nonetheless, wherever he hangs his hat—on a coat rack near a front door or on a peg in a mudroom (his hats: a couple of battered baseball caps, a boater he's held on to, a more recently acquired acrylic knit cap by which to get through the winters)—he outfits the kitchen with the basic utensils plus a few others that catch his eye when he's up and down Williams-Sonoma aisles or the like. That's if the basic utensils are not already *in situ*.

He doesn't import much else. Of course, he unboxes his books and places them on the library's shelves but only after contacting a painter whose phone number he finds on a photocopied piece of paper taped to a pole near his front door. He positions a few framed paintings, prints and photographs here and there. In the library, and for a reason he can't peg, he keeps a photograph of himself on the Carson show, autographed by Carson or by someone authorized to forge Carson's name. "Never upstage me again," it says. (Elihu is convinced jokester Carson, or the minion to whom he left such signing chores, was only half-joking.) He hangs framed drawings of his first-edition dust jackets. In the past when he's done that, he has taken them down on a passing whim and then put them up again when the whim passed in the opposite direction. He is well aware the whims could recur. On the right end table by the four-poster in the second-floor back bedroom, he has set a framed photograph of him with his arm around Bartlett Norcross. How young they look. They are standing side by side. Bart, on the left, is looking at Elihu, his profile reporting a neatly chiseled jawline. Elihu, on the right, is looking directly at the camera. That face is the one he didn't used to mind when he spied it in a mirror. From time to time, he even got a kick out of it. Both Elihu, in his Eli days, and Bart, in his Bart days, are smiling broadly.

V.

Not knowing why the photograph is there isn't quite right. What's right is he doesn't *want* to know why. What's even righter is he doesn't want to admit to himself that he knows why. He has perversely placed the photograph, taken in the early 1980s (it must be the spring of 1982). His placement of it, without his having removed it since then, may explain, if only to some extent, why he sleeps so infrequently in the four-poster.

Guilt. It's guilt. He knows he has done the wrong thing in relation to Bartlett, whom friends called Bart. Bartlett himself insisted he be called Bart. He disliked the given name Bartlett because he said it made him sound like a pear. He said his mother insisted that if he thought he sounded like a pear, then he sounded like a sweet pear, because, Mrs. Norcross said, that's what Bartlett pears are. Bart disagreed, claiming that anyone hearing the name Bartlett before meeting him would expect someone pear-shaped.

Elihu had a different theory, a theory he chose not to present to Bartlett. To Bart. He believed Bartlett preferred Bart because it had more of a regular-guy ring to it. He suspected Bart considered the name Bartlett Norcross as sounding just the tiniest bit hoity-toity, "Bartlett" also being a family name. As a gay man still slightly ashamed he was gay, though he would never concede as much, he liked being just plain Bart Norcross.

Elihu's knowing this, or being convinced he's known this, is at the core of his guilt where Bart is concerned. He believes that his leaving Bart is a negative judgment on Bart's homosexuality. He believes that his breaking off the relationship—okay, the love affair (Bart had no doubt it was a love affair)—was for Bart substantiation that being gay is less than. This is a reiteration of what Bart's father, Christian Norcross, had maintained, not in so many words but in those exact, abrasive words.

To the contrary, though, Elihu is aware that he'd ended the idyll with Bart not in judgment of Bart. Who was he to sit in judgment of Bart's sexuality? To each his own. He ended the relationship in response to his own extensive deliberations. He had come to the decision after much discussion, with himself and with Bart (whom he so often and silently thought of as Bartlett), that he, Elihu, was finally not comfortable living as homosexual, or even as bisexual.

He had enjoyed living with Bart, who was twelve years younger than he, who had the blonde, blue-eyed looks of a patrician Protestant, who had a thriving pediatrician's practice with the concomitant income, and who possessed a great sense of humor when not taking himself too seriously. Elihu had even derived pleasure from their sexual encounters, from their lovemaking.

He'd genuinely enjoyed pleasure in certain practices that when carried on—when carried out—didn't really affect him as that different in sensation from heterosexual activity. On the other hand, no pun intended, he had never felt completely at ease with it. It wasn't just that he never completely accustomed himself to fellatio, to sucking cock. He simply could never persuade himself he was involved in anything more than an extended experiment that eventually impressed him as reverting to mother's nipple, a regression that interested him more than anything else—well, maybe not more than anything else but rather that at bottom. Also, no pun intended, it hinted more deeply at some infantilizing need in him he ultimately found retrograde. Yes, that's it: retrograde.

Long before he met Bart, he had expounded on a writer's obligation to try everything. (Everything within reason, that is; murder is uncalled for.) Otherwise, one must confess to being deficient as a writer—on the odd occasion he continued thinking of himself as a writer. There is nothing else he could consider himself as, is there, despite regarding himself as a writer who chose no longer to write and lived by the choice with a skimpy modicum of contentment.

The rationale—his discomfort living as homosexual—on which basis Elihu contended that Bart and he should end the affair, was one thing. That he knew Bart didn't believe him (though the sincere fellow made a show of pretending he did) was another thing entirely. Tougher for Elihu to accept, even fleetingly, was his realizing Bart regarded their parting as not Elihu's fault, if fault is the right word, but his own. Bart saw it, not incorrectly, as Elihu's ultimately going for the heterosexual life over the homosexual. That was visibly devastating for Bart, who took the break as confirmation of his less-than assessment of himself.

Elihu knew he might have taken that fact into account, though he didn't see how it could be done without capitulating to Bart. Still, the persistent inkling that there existed a better way to go about it is the basis for his guilt and for his keeping the photograph of Bart and him in happy times—relatively happier times—on the bedside table. Yes, it must be why, in some small or large way, he doesn't spend many nights in that bed.

Also, Elihu has to face up to his interlude with Bart being relatively happy for a time, whereas happiness, even short-lived, was not a standard occurrence in his past peregrinating decades. Maybe his placing the framed picture by his bed has more to do with that and less to do with guilt than he thinks. Maybe Elihu's positioning of the picture on the bedside table is a reminder he isn't ready to admit to himself he lacks the ability to find happiness. Put in another perspective, maybe the photograph is a reminder of his continuing inability to find happiness for any length of time.

Maybe the photograph is his way of reminding himself about the power that ambiguity wields over a life. With that, he is familiar.

Sizing up the nature of his time with Bart, Elihu was aware he was assigning the interval a Freudian interpretation. He knew Freud had fallen out of favor in the eighties, but he was never a man for society's silly vicissitudes and wasn't going to alter his outlook now. Hadn't he been living according to those convictions for going on thirty years?

vi.

Within weeks of Elihu's having taken up residence at 73 East Ninth Street and furnishing the place as much as he was inclined to—taking furniture he had in storage, picking up a few serviceable pieces at Housing Thrift Works and Angel Street Thrift Shop—he's fallen into a loose routine. The routines he establishes wherever he has lived over the past decades are always loose. There is never any reason for them to be strict. When in what he considers his dim past, in the days when he was writing, he hewed to a strict regimen. He woke early, no later than five-thirty in the morning, showered, brewed strong coffee, drank it along with toasted English muffins and jam of some sort. Then he wrote until noon on the Smith-Corona Jean and Morris had given him when he left for his Yale freshman year. He allowed no interruptions. He answered no phone calls. He responded to no doorbell ring. He rarely even rose from the chair. If he were stuck for a word or a thought, he might get up and pace for a minute or two, let the word or thought come to him and sit again.

He never rid himself of the Smith-Corona. It goes with him to every new house or apartment or country cottage, where it is immediately stowed at the back of a closet. He had it repaired whenever it needed repairing—at shops that existed in good numbers then, less so now, when, thank goodness, he doesn't need them. The abandoned Smith-Corona and a few accompanying reams of foolscap are lodged in one of the low library-study cabinets. There they rest along with *Wandering Youth* and *For My Betters* drafts that he also can't bring himself to toss into a bin but that he also refuses to donate or sell to importuning collections housed at, for instance, Yale's Beinecke Library. Each time he moves house he packs and unpacks the manuscripts and asks himself the same question: "Why do I hold on to these?" He never comes up with a satisfactory answer. Nor does he come up with a satisfactory answer why he cannot bring himself to toss them or, better yet, shred them or, much better yet, burn them.

Now the updated and loose routine he follows includes breakfast and lunch, which he usually takes at home, and dinner at one of the nearby restaurants where he favors dark corners. He patronizes no restaurant with lighted corners. For exercise he takes at least two walks a day within a ten-block radius, attempting, and usually succeeding, in never stopping for a red light. He reads *The New York Times* in the morning and most weeks picks up a periodical like *The New Yorker*, *The Economist*, *The New York Review of Books*. (He never takes a subscription. He doesn't want to find himself filling out change-of-address forms.) He peruses them, but often, when an article fails to make a meaningful point, he throws the offending thing aside. Later, he picks up the magazine from where it lies and puts it in the hemp basket he has purchased to set by the club chair. He empties it every couple of weeks. He spends four or five hours of the day reading, but not necessarily the same four or five hours. (When reading, he turns Handel down but not off.) Some afternoons and some evenings he walks to movie houses close by and, not having determined before he left the house what he wants to see, checks the marquee and buys a ticket for whatever is starting soonest. He finds whatever he chooses entertaining or meaningful to a degree but mostly just lets the movie wash over him. There was one feature during which a sufficiently wise character said, "Fiction is worthless." He had to agree with that. He never goes to the theater. Going to the theater requires arriving at an appointed hour. He objects to appointed hours. He wants all his hours to be flexible, unspoken for, deliberately unlike the cramped, demanding hours of his vanishing (his vanished) past.

Since he moved into 73 East Ninth Street in November (on November tenth to be exact), he arrived only two weeks before Thanksgiving and only about six weeks before Christmas and, for that matter, Chanukah. He celebrates none of them but does try not to give in to annoyance over their omnipresence. On Thanksgiving, he has dinner on Waverly Place and orders turkey. Why not? He likes turkey, if for nothing else than the supposedly nourishing tryptophan and the cranberry sauce. More than once as Christmas approaches with lights everywhere, with decorated trees everywhere, with carols broadcast everywhere, he thinks about not exhibiting any out-and-out Scrooge-like traits. He satisfies himself that his was not the only house on the block evidencing no Christmas tree (as well as no Chanukah bush) inside, no candles in the window or wreath on the door. He even entertains the thought that had he been the only house on the block without candles in the window or a wreath on the door, he might have given in to adding them for the sole purpose of not wanting to call attention to himself. Luckily, there's no need. On New Year's Eve, he is aware of people blowing horns in the street. He can even hear a hum from Washington Square. He hears it at the back of the house, in the library-study as he intermittently looks up from *The Magic Mountain*, which he is rereading for the fifth or sixth time.

Why the constant rereading? Is it not obvious? Firstly, reading and rereading distract him from thinking about himself, from enumerating the reasons behind his self-imposed predicament, from dwelling on his endless plight. Secondly, he rereads to remind himself what truly good writing is, how it formidably contrasts with what he published. Perhaps he'll finally learn something. To apply to what? To apply to nothing.

Looking out the window on the dark garden, he sees no sign of the snowfall that had been forecast. He goes to bed at eleven o'clock on, not in, the convertible bed nearest the club chair, pulling over himself one of the two Pendleton blankets he bought for the convertible beds as a Christmas/Chanukah treat. See, he tells himself, he doesn't completely dismiss the holiday spirit. He sleeps as soundly as he ever has, waking once to go downstairs to piss and once from a dream that instantly evaporated. Both times he notices the silence outside and is grateful for it.

More broadly, he is grateful for January. When he was younger, he had always disliked January for its grey, dry, dingy quality, the reminder that holiday joy had been drained from it. When in colder climes during his first few decades, he habitually longed for January and equally grey, dispiriting February to be over. Valentine's Day? Ha! Now he likes the two months for those very dulling things. January requires no response. To his way of thinking, January leaves you alone. So does February. Being left alone is what he desires most.

The appreciation of being left entirely to his own modest, shrunken devices, had almost deterred him from returning to the city. Had he gone, when he decided to vacate Bedford, to some of the places where he'd contemplated putting down (weak) roots, he knew he wouldn't be taking the risks to which he would expose himself in New York City, in Manhattan. The risks, of course, boiled down to one all-encompassing risk: running into people he knows—that is, running into people he knew. He had known many people in Manhattan. Relatives, yes, but even more so, friends, other writers, publishers, school chums, old girlfriends, old lovers (e.g., Bart Norcross).

Yet, following extended deliberation he decided to come back. It had been twenty-five years or thereabouts. He regarded it as a challenge. He would return to New York on the condition that he avoid reminders of his previous life there. (He likes that he cannot recall exactly when he had last vacated the intense, infernal, inescapable city.) He would employ tactics such as seeking out those restaurants with dark corners, such as crossing the street should he spot an old acquaintance coming his way.

He knows that crossing streets at the sight of someone, anyone, he wants to avoid would only be effective if he does the spotting first. It's paramount that he be vigilant. The ten-block-radius walk is part of the strategy. The limited area includes the Strand Book Store, which, on the one hand, is convenient for his regular practice of buying books, but on the other hand, is a venue where he might very well see people (readers, authors) he has known. A baseball cap pulled low over his brow is a partial solution.

But only partial. One overcast, snow-threatening February day, he is in the fiction section (P-S) searching for a Richard Prince novel when, looking up at a higher shelf and thereby exposing his face, he hears "Elihu? Eli, is that you?" His first instinct is to ignore the question and the somewhat familiar male voice. Rather, he would walk briskly away from whence the voice is emanating. He can't bring himself to do that, not when he realizes how close the person is and that acting as if he had heard nothing isn't feasible. He is annoyed that he hadn't thought to keep his head low. He might have been able to do that by climbing the ladder only one or two feet away.

He hasn't safeguarded himself accordingly. So he turns. The voice sounded familiar to him and is. He didn't instantly identify it. He wouldn't have instantly identified it. He hadn't heard it for maybe thirty years and even then hadn't known its owner all that well.

"I thought it was you, Eli," the man says. It's the novelist Charles Hornsby, whose first novels were released at about the same time as Elihu's. The two men had been considered for some of the same prizes, were often seated on the same panels, were present at the same literary lunches, held aloft drinks at the same publishing parties. Their acquaintance did date back to Elihu, to Eli days. Hence the (unappreciated) "Eli" salutation. They had never been friends. Elihu had never thought much of Hornsby's writing. He was well aware that Hornsby had kept the novels coming, but when Elihu has seen the latest Charles Hornsby work while browsing in a bookstore wherever he was living, he has never done more than pick it up to scan the dust jacket or maybe read an opening sentence or paragraph to confirm his negative opinion.

"Charles," he says with enough verve to disguise his disappointment, his annoyance with himself, his utter lack of interest.

"That's Chuck to you," Hornsby says. As a young man, Hornsby had always been tall, thin, reedy. He had a thin face with a pronounced chin, and had a habit of jutting it out, as if intent on expressing undue pride in himself. He had always dressed well. He is well-dressed now in a smart Chesterfield overcoat and the sort of wide-brimmed fedora few men still wore. Since Elihu had seen Hornsby last (at who knows what event), he has put on weight. He has put on years, too. Noticing the weight and the weight of years makes Elihu aware of his own added years.

Thinking "I'm thinking he looks old, and he's thinking I look old," Elihu—abruptly and once again Eli—doesn't jump at the chance to amend his measured greeting to Chuck. Hornsby takes up the slack. "I haven't seen you in dog years, Eli. I can't remember where I heard you were living last. Are you living here now?"

Hornsby's chin is doing its jutting act, and he is smiling a toothy smile that Elihu recognizes but realizes he had forgotten. Hornsby—Chuck—is waiting for an answer. Elihu is at a brief loss for how to respond. He does not like the idea of lying outright, but if he even says he is living in Manhattan for the time being, he worries about the consequences. "Yes, but I don't know for how long. I needed to take care of a few things I can only do here." He is being deliberately vague. He hopes that will do.

"In that case," Hornsby says, "we've got to get together. Soon. I know Florrie would love to see you."

Florrie. He is talking about Florence, his wife. She is Florrie Hornsby now, but when Elihu first knew her, she was Florence Robbins. When she was Florence Robbins and a reporter for a local news station, he had gone out with her. That is something else Hornsby and he had in common. When they were young, younger, they'd both gone out with the same woman. There cannot be said to have been a rivalry. For most of the time, Florence had been mum about whom she was seeing. At the time, Eli—he was Eli to Florrie, too—knew there was someone else, but he didn't know who, nor did he much care. He had liked Florrie, whom he met when she came to interview him about the publication of *For My Betters*. She was smart and funny. She was certainly good-looking without making a big deal about it, but in those busy days he was enjoying what was happening to him too much to think about tying himself down. He did anything but think about tying himself down. Florrie wasn't ready to tie herself down, either, at least not with him. Only when she ended a relationship that was not committed enough to call a relationship—theirs—did she suggest to Eli that he was not "husband material." (He was only too happy to admit she was right about that. She wasn't the first nor was she the last to offer the opinion.) It was after they'd agreed to be friends, lovers no more, that he learned Florrie had been dating Charles Hornsby at the same time. Virtually on alternate nights. Apparently, Charles Hornsby *was* "husband material." He also came to learn that Hornsby knew about Florrie and him all along. That explained the especially pronounced Hornsby chin-jut during those salad days.

"How is Florrie?" he asks.

"She's fine," Hornsby says, "if you don't count the arthritis. Minor arthritis, she'd want me to stress. Now that you're back, I know she'd love to see you."

This is getting to be too much for Elihu. The idea of social obligations nearly makes him squirm. "As I say, Charles, I don't know how long I'm back for." His thought to himself is that many more, *any more*, meetings like this one and he will not be back for very long at all. He leavens the thought with acknowledging to himself that he has been at 73 East Ninth for more than three months, and encountering Charles Hornsby is the first time he has not avoided what he expressly had set out to avoid. Perhaps he should count himself lucky and make a point of being even more circumspect in the future, in whatever New York City future he is going to have.

Hornsby is going on. "Florrie would love to see you, Eli, and I'd like the chance to catch up as well. Find out where you've been, what you're working on, fill you in on what I'm up to."

Ay, there's the rub. In Hornsby's case, it's not so much the rub as the rubbing it in. Hornsby knows, or if he doesn't know, he surely suspects that while he's turning out a book every year or every year and a half—as if he is on an assembly line—Elihu is writing nothing. At best, as far as Hornsby can surmise, Elihu is writing nothing for publication. Hornsby has to have suspected as much. There has been no new book for so long. Not for a quarter of a century. He can almost smell the envy and vindictive triumph behind the held smile and the chin presentation. He well knows that as a result of nothing he had deliberately engineered, the early literary attentions accorded him had had the effect of sidelining other young authors. Hornsby had been one of their slighted number and, it is still evident, would never get over it. Decades earlier, he had made plain that his victory over Elihu in the matter of Florrie was some consolation but hardly enough. Nothing would ever be enough. Elihu might have been tempted to see Florrie again. To discern after all this time whether she might reveal something positive or negative about her nuptial choice is an inviting notion, but he recognizes a cheap incentive in himself when it pops up. Furthermore, he likes his instinctive—he'll dub it valor—his instinctive valor to dismiss it. More than that, an evening when he has nothing to say as they deal in pleasantries while masking lingering resentments is more than he wants to take in, much less take on.

This hesitant moment—Hornsby's looking him squarely, expectantly in the face the way he is—is exactly what Elihu does not want. Hornsby isn't letting him off the hook. His Chesterfield is open and he's patting the pockets of a double-breasted blue blazer for a wallet. When he locates it, he pulls out a business card. "I can't remember if you ever had our number," he says, handing Elihu the card. "Either way, here it is." He pulls a look of sincerity that Elihu takes as too sincere to be anything but insincere. He knows the invitation is sincere, but whether Hornsby knows it consciously, the reason underlying the invitation is not. No matter. Elihu won't act on it were it completely unalloyed, if only because he is no longer their Eli and hasn't been for some long time.

All the same, he accepts the card. Refusing would be childish, churlish. Taking it, he says nothing. He knows Hornsby is waiting for him to say something. "Thanks." "I'll call you." "Say hello to Florrie for me." Anything along those lines. When Hornsby realizes nothing of the sort is imminent, he says, "Give us a ring. I mean it."

Elihu says nothing to that. He hopes Hornsby gets the message couched in the silence. He thinks Hornsby might have. He also thinks he might not have. Whether yes or no, the most Elihu gives the repeated offer is a boyish shrug.

Hornsby sees the shrug. He can't miss it, but he doesn't acknowledge it. He just pats Elihu on the shoulder, says he has to get going, turns and hustles off.

Elihu realizes he has just been transparently rude but accepts his unpleasantness as necessary if he is to keep to his be-no-social-prisoner policy. He takes a few seconds to recall that he is where he is to find the Richard Prince novel. Making a show to himself of sloughing off Hornsby's unsolicited interruption, he returns to the task he had set himself and completes it. He pulls the Prince novel from the shelf and assures himself that he has a quiet, unimposed-on evening of reading in front of him.

vii.

Elihu is in the shower on a later dismal February morning. He is enjoying the showerhead power. These are the things that give him enjoyment. If fleeting. Perhaps *because* fleeting. In the three-months-plus he's been in the house, having workmen in to improve things like the showerhead (when those sorts of endeavors are beyond his D.I.Y. skills), this kind of daily ritual is how he spends time when he isn't reading, eating or sleeping. He has had a plumber, two electricians (he was dissatisfied with the first one), a wallpaper hanger. (He hadn't shopped for wallpaper. He found rolls in a library-study cabinet that matched the faded wallpaper already there and decided to have it refreshed.) He has consulted no one about whom to hire. In walking around the neighborhood, he has seen businesses. For the wallpaper hanger, he pulled a phone number for "an affable jack-of-all-trades at moderate prices" from yet another sheet of paper taped to a pole at a nearby corner. (The neighborhood poles have been invaluable consultants.) He cared nothing for the promise of affability. "Affability" indicated an unwanted inclination to talk. He did like the "moderate prices" part. As much as he can, he avoids the big-city gouging he sees everywhere.

As he showers, he glimpses the reflection of his soaped body in the cabinet mirror every few seconds. He is used to the ravages, which doesn't mean he accepts them. He's pissed off about them, but by now the only response to his naked frame—indisputably five feet ten inches in the halcyon days, though, he suspects, now more like five feet nine inches—is a quickly furrowed brow, a shrug, a silent "So what?"

Above the rush of water, he thinks he hears the front-door buzzer.

He's not certain, and even if he were, he would ignore it. He isn't expecting anyone. Aside from Mrs. Woolard and the (not that many) delivery men and women and service people over the last months, he has expected no one in the time he has been at 73 East Ninth Street. The solitude (putting Handel aside) is soothing, precious. He wants nothing to compromise it. He is determined nothing will compromise it.

Continuing his shower, he again thinks he hears the front-door buzzer. (He would have disconnected the buzzer if he had not determined there were times when it is a necessary intrusion.) Then he thinks he hears the lion's-head knocker. He steps out of the shower to towel himself off amid the stuffy, dying steam. Now he knows he hears the buzzer and the knocker. He stands still with the towel pulled over the grey-and-white pelt on his chest. He hears both again.

He continues drying. He decides to assume that whoever is buzzing and knocking repeatedly will eventually realize he or she has come to the wrong house and go away.

He finishes drying, puts on a clean pair of boxers, the black T-shirt and khaki trousers he's been wearing for the last week and slips into his down-at-heel loafers.

Having done that, having run a brush through his hair without looking at himself in the mirror, he realizes that the front-door disturbances that had almost slipped his mind have ceased while he was thinking about returning to James Joyce's *Ulysses*, another classic he rereads at least once a decade. Yes, that's what writing should be!

Instead of returning to the library-study immediately, he thinks he'll check the front door to make certain that whoever had been doing all but banging on it has gone. He walks down the stairs, not avoiding, as he never does, the creaking steps he has memorized by now. He goes into the living room for a good view of the brownstone stoop.

He pulls back—but no more than an inch—one of the white curtains he let hang loose when he assumed occupancy. He'd left them that way to discourage inquisitive pedestrians. Now he's disappointed to see that while the buzzing and knocking have stopped, the stoop is occupied.

Sitting on the third step up from the sidewalk with his feet planted on the first step and with his back to the front door is what appears to be a young man. He is wearing a black parka, has a bloated backpack on and has placed a medium-sized suitcase on wheels, handle raised, on the pavement in front of him. A scuffed military duffel bag leans against it.

The young man is peering directly in front of him. Due to the angle at which he is sitting, Elihu cannot tell much about the young man's looks. When after a few seconds, the young man slowly, even languidly, looks right and left, as if deciding what to do next, Elihu has a better view of someone with broad features, a high brow, black eyes. a slightly hooked nose, full lips, a pronounced cleft chin.

Suddenly, as if the young man senses he is being watched, he looks towards the window where Elihu hovers furtively. Elihu lets the curtain fall back in place. He feels foolish. It's possible (likely?) the young man saw him. It's even likelier the young man saw the curtain move and realizes he has been seen. Carelessly, Elihu has revealed that someone is home. The young man may resume ringing the doorbell, may resume assaulting the knocker.

Were he to do that, Elihu could continue ignoring the intrusion, but making a snap decision, he preempts the buzzer. He preempts the knocker. He goes to the door. He unlocks the three locks he has had installed and opens the door.

He guessed right about the young man's insistence. He has stood and climbed two of the stairs. He stops where he is.

Elihu sees a young man he judges to be about five feet ten inches.

He appears to be stocky—somewhere around two hundred twenty pounds, Elihu gauges—but the parka could be lending him girth. He's not a bad-looking young man, though at the moment he's wearing a quizzical expression, almost imitating a mask of comedy.

The face is familiar. Elihu knows he can easily place it. He doesn't complete the thought because the young man speaks. "Excuse me," he says in a young man's gruff voice, the voice of a young man who has only recently grown into that voice. "I'm looking for Elihu Goulding."

Because Elihu knows, or strongly suspects, what's going on, he doesn't want to address the naked reality of it immediately. The physical resemblance is too pressing between this young man and the young man Elihu saw in the mirror a few decades back. Instead, he says with, he hopes, no affect, "I am Elihu Goulding. Who's asking?"

His response springs from his just short of absolute certainty about who this young man is.

The young man has taken another step up and is extending his right hand. "My name is Ethan Haas. My mother is Emily Haas. You're my father."

This is the answer Elihu expects. The minute he looked the young man in the face, the minute he saw the unmistakable features, he knew who this young man had to be. It was not as if he had always known this day would come, and here it is. The opposite. He had figured—he had been led to believe—it would never come.

But as if predestined, it had come, and for the moment the only thing he thinks he can do is shake the young man's—Ethan Haas's—outstretched hand. He does. The feel of this young man's hand in his, this grip, is unlike any handshake he has ever experienced. It's as if he is shaking hands with himself.

viii.

Elihu and Ethan are sitting downstairs at the table in the kitchen. It's a table just this side of rickety he found at a Goodwill Store on Eighth Avenue and brought home in a taxi. He'd been hoping to find one like it and considered himself lucky when he did. It reminds him of the table Jean had in the kitchen on Academy Street when he was growing up. That's why he felt lucky. Not just to find it. His satisfaction is due to Jean herself considering her wooden table lucky. Always claiming she was not at all superstitious and that she regarded superstitions as "a waste of time and energy," she would rap the aging, ageless wooden table with the knuckles of her left hand when something occurred she sensed could use luck—any reference, more often than not, to good health or to the prospect of money coming in.

Laughing wryly at himself for attempting to replicate his mother's attitude towards luck, Elihu is glad to have the table. For him it has, in a phrase he normally disdains, "sentimental value." What kind of value is that? He prides himself on equating sentimental value with no value whatsoever. At the same time as he figures himself a fool for claiming to have a lucky table—or a stand-in for a lucky table—he admits to himself he has gone out of his way to locate it and has no intention of getting rid of it.

He regards it as a keeper, in spite of his belief that there is no such thing as luck. No, that's not quite it. He suspects there might be something that qualifies as luck, but he is not certain what the something is. He doesn't see that luck has had much to do with his life, not when so many things he thought were lucky were eventually revealed as the opposite. Examples? What about his entire writing career? What, at the end of the day, had been so lucky about that? The commercial rewards allowing him to live a life free from financial care? Insufficient proof. Mightn't he have achieved that status had his life gone in any number of other directions? Anyway, what kind of a life has he had? Does he have?

And yet here the kitchen table is, from now on a constant reminder, he has to acknowledge to himself on a regular basis, that he holds out Jean's deluding hope. The persistent thought crosses his mind at least once while he sits opposite Ethan Haas, who has taken off his parka and the two thick sweaters he'd worn rather than packed. He'd hung all three items on the wooden coat rack Elihu had bought for the entrance area. He has also taken off the mud-covered boots he had on, revealing thick grey athletic socks that looked as if they, too, like everything Ethan is wearing and like Ethan himself, could stand laundering.

Ethan is now down to a third bulky Irish cabled sweater, under which is a polo shirt, and heavy military green trousers with various zippered and buckled pockets. He still carries the thick smell of the road. He is ravenously eating the scrambled eggs and buttered toast and gulping the caffeinated coffee Elihu has whipped up for him. For the uninvited meeting, Elihu had tested the limits of his culinary skills. When he lives in the country, knowing how to cook the basics and not anything requiring a recipe found in one of Jean's cookbooks often beats driving miles to restaurants. When he lives in the city, the occasional scrambled eggs or chicken soup with rice cuts down on going out to restaurants where he might be seen by people whom he does not want to be seen by, dark corners or no dark corners.

Because Ethan is eating as if there's no tomorrow and as if his recent yesterdays were underfed, Elihu is carrying on most of the conversation. When there is conversation. Much of the hour or less since Ethan arrived has passed in silence, during which Elihu has scrutinized this boy who claims to be his son, who is, without contradiction, his son—this despite Ethan, in his introduction, referring to Elihu as his father but not adding anything to the effect of "I'm your son."

No, Ethan had not yet said he is Elihu's son. He hasn't yet used the word, a distinction Elihu notes. Ethan and he resemble each other so strongly that his questioning their biological connection at all strikes him as bordering on cowardice, a dereliction of duties he never expected to fill. How extensively he will need to fulfill them is unclear. So far, he sees this mid-morning breakfast as perhaps the only undisputed requirement. So far, it is only incumbent on him to agree he is Ethan's father. It's a matter of DNA that Elihu sees no reason to test. But son? To him that designation carries connotations beyond anything he and Ethan have approached.

"Does your mother know where you are?" Elihu asks when Ethan has paused between mouthfuls.

He waits for a response and takes those many seconds to look at this boy, whom he has learned is twenty-one—"almost twenty-two," a qualification Elihu finds intriguing in a young man long past such a childish remark. This is information he already has. He knows when Ethan was born. Elihu knows full well when he was with—but emphatically *not in love with*—Emily Haas.

ix.

Elihu was in his early forties and in Chicago. On that particular relocation, he had thought it would be fun—as if he ever did anything he would admit was strictly fun—to study informally at the University of Chicago, to audit classes, to get a brief taste of a University of Chicago education, about which he and the rest of the world had long heard so much.

He met Emily Haas at a Saul Bellow lecture, no less. Not exactly at a lecture, but on leaving a lecture, when, passing through a door to the street, she fumbled with the doorknob and dropped her books. Looking back on that now, as he had occasionally looked back on it in the past, he regards the meet-cute aspect of it just this side of too cloying to acknowledge.

Worse, one of the books he helped her retrieve, against her demurrals as they both bent down, was his novel, was *Wandering Youth*. When she had her five or so books relatively secured, he had time to look her over. She was close to his height, had auburn hair, which, along with Elihu's facial attributes, he recognized that Ethan had inherited from her, one of the few attributes the boy had inherited from her. Ethan wore it now almost as long as she had then. She wore her hair shoulder length and pulled back with a rubber band. (Ethan dispensed with the rubber band.) She had piercing blue eyes and amusingly curved lips. Because she was wearing a shapeless raincoat, he couldn't tell much about her figure but instantly wanted to know more.

Seeing the bestseller that had brought him such eventually dashed returns, he said, disingenuously, "I see you're reading *Wandering Youth*. What do you think of it?"

Raising her full eyebrows, she said, "It's okay, I guess. As far as I've gotten."

They had stopped on the venerable Cobb Hall steps. Elihu said, "Just okay? I heard it was pretty good."

She raised an eyebrow and said, "You heard it from men, I bet. I'm not convinced women like it. Elihu Goulding still has plenty to learn about women, or did when he wrote it. I'm reading it mainly because Bellow recommended it. With a few funny reservations. Not that Bellow has room to talk. He still has plenty to learn about women, too. He runs through wives as if they were Kleenex. And I don't know if you've noticed this, but with the women in the classroom, he can be very flirtatious. At the same time as he's curt with the men."

Elihu noticed she assumed he had been in the lecture hall or perhaps had actually spotted him there. He also thought to himself that she did run on. "I didn't notice that," Elihu said. "Is he?" Intent on fishing for more *Wandering Youth* aperçus from this obviously bright, obviously good-looking, obviously undergraduate, he asked, "I'm interested in anything else you have to say about the Goulding book. As far as you've gotten. I've been meaning to read it myself, Miss. Or is it Ms.? Uh…well, I don't know your name."

Emily fumbled with her books again, put out her free right hand and said, "I'm Emily Haas." They shook hands. "And you're?"

For Elihu, this was a tricky moment. He'd put himself in a position where he couldn't say, "I'm the author we're discussing. I'm Elihu Goulding." Near as he could grope, he would have to give a fictitious name, but whereas he had been facile at dreaming up names for his fiction—when, that is, he was still writing fiction—he was momentarily lost for words, for manufactured names.

After several seconds elapsed, Emily looked Elihu directly in the eyes and said, matter of factly, *too* matter of factly for Elihu, "No need to tell me your name. I know it. You're Elihu Goulding." She pointed at her books. "Have you forgotten your photo is on the dust jacket?"

"Yes," Elihu said, "but it was taken a long time ago. I don't look like that anymore."

"Actually, you do," Emily Haas said. "Maybe a few years older, but you still look a lot like you looked when this picture was taken by—." Fumbling with the book, she turned it over and read, "Jill Krementz. By Jill Krementz." She held up the photograph for him to check out. "It may not be the smartest idea to go around pretending you aren't who you are. You only embarrass yourself."

It was at that moment when Elihu had an epiphany—and had Emily Haas to thank for it. He realized something he should have reckoned long before. He realized that just because he no longer felt like his former twenties-thirties self, it didn't mean that at forty-two, he no longer looked like himself. He could no longer deny who he was just because he had come to believe shuffling off that tiresome part of his mental mortal coil meant his visible mortal coil had also not stayed identifiably intact.

Attempting to recover lost ground, he forced a small laugh and said, "I guess you got me. I am the mortified Elihu Goulding." For some reason he tacked on, while withholding a bow, "At your service."

"That's nice of you to say, Mr. Goulding," Emily Haas said, making as if to go, "but at the moment, I don't require any servicing."

Along with a perfume of breeziness Elihu was getting from Emily Haas, he also detected a strong whiff of independence, a trait he liked in women. And men, too—men who he had long since ascertained may have prided themselves on being independent but were often indisputably not, were woefully dependent on any number of real or imagined things.

As he viewed it, independence in women usually meant, if it was genuine, he wouldn't become depended upon by them—"Not husband material," another way of phrasing it.

"In that case, what would you say to a cup of coffee?" he said to Emily Haas. He could see her weighing what in her mind might be the pros and cons. "That's if you have the time. I don't mean to crowd you, but I'd be interested in what you think of Bellow as a teacher. And as a novelist."

"And as something of a contemporary?" Emily Haas said, again raising her eyebrow and her inflection.

"Oh, no, no," Elihu replied. "I don't consider Saul Bellow a contemporary. Perhaps I would if I were still writing. I'm not. I do not write anymore." He said the last sentence with heightened force, as he'd come to do whenever he felt it necessary to insist on his current and, he resolutely believed, future status.

"It's true then?" Emily Haas said, and Elihu thought he spotted a hither-to absent interest. "When Bellow talked about *Wandering Youth* a few weeks ago, he said there were rumors you have stopped writing. He said he hoped they weren't true. He said he was always sorry when promising writers didn't fulfill their promise."

"Promise?" Elihu leaped on the word faster than he meant to. Did this indicate the opinion Saul Bellow held of him was as "promising"? Only that, nothing more? It wasn't that he regarded Bellow—whom he admired (why else would he be living temporarily in Chicago and auditing Bellow's class?)—as the final arbiter on his novels. It was worse. It was that, without rereading *Wandering Youth*, *For My Betters* and *The Accidental Immigrants*—he knew their contents, for Pete's sake—he had come to the same conclusion. He had called a halt to his writing because he believed that, yes, he had been "promising" but that *The Accidental Immigrants* demonstrated he would be unable to build on that promise. It was as if he had just learned what for some time he had expected to have confirmed about himself. And he had just learned it from as authoritative an arbiter as might come along: Saul Bellow. Okay, not directly from Bellow but an apparently reliable source. It was as if this were the true purpose of his surreptitious auditing, surreptitious because he always sat in the back of the auditorium on the slim chance Bellow might recognize him no matter how he thought he no longer looked like the earlier, then renowned Elihu Goulding. (They had only met once, at an American Book Association conference.) Bellow's dismissal was confirmation of his own refusal to reread any of his three novels. Because now, decades on, he would recognize himself as promising and no more than that. He was concerned he would come to a worse conclusion: that he would judge himself as not even having risen to what he considered "promising."

"I suppose I could go for coffee," Emily Haas said after a few seconds during which Elihu had the impression she'd been musing on his silence. Could she be intrigued by his response, whatever it was, to what they'd just been saying? As if she wanted to know more about those responses—as if (could this be?) she was able to guess at them.

Trying to disguise any misgivings he had hinted, he decided to be chipper. He said, "Coffee, it is. Where can we go? I don't know the local hot spots yet."

"There's always Starbucks," Emily said. "They're popping up all over the place, and the coffee is good, or was when they started out."

They went to the nearest Starbucks, and that's how began an episode that, like many other episodes in Elihu's life, was sweet before becoming, in his view (the only view that counted for him), bittersweet.

After having a break-the-remaining-ice talk at Starbucks, Elihu offered to take Emily to dinner. She said she had papers she needed to write but could be free the following night, a Friday, and "would enjoy dinner with you…I think." He liked the "I think" and the short pause that preceded it.

She did allow him to walk her to the house where, she explained, she shared rooms with two other students. When they reached the front door, she extended her hand before he'd decided whether to try kissing her. He had been watching her mouth while she spoke and had judged it an enticing mouth—those artistically curved lips—but now realized he had better shake her hand. Not a complete loss, he assessed, as he'd also liked her hands and the graceful way she used them when she spoke.

Having put the books down, they shook hands, Elihu holding on a few seconds longer to make an unspoken point. When he did, she looked down at their clasped hands, letting him know she got it, that she got the flirtatious intent. She withdrew her hand, picked up the books, said goodbye, turned quickly and, without turning back for a parting look, went inside. Elihu thought that he might have helped with the books or offered to hold the door open. Too late.

Something about anticipation is that while it can so often outstrip reality, every once in a while it underestimates reality. Elihu had that stray insight when he'd rung Emily's doorbell the following night and had been asked up to the apartment she was sharing. It didn't escape Elihu's notice that both roommates found reason to pass through the living room to get a look at the still-somewhat-famous author gracing their digs. One of them told him she had read *Wandering Youth* in her senior year at New Trier and thought it was "really, really good, *really* good."

Was it Joyce who said that or Jennifer? Elihu never did get Emily's "roomies" straight in the few months Emily and he were, er, an item. Whichever it was sitting cross-legged in her sweats on a sofa that had seen better days, she said if she'd had her copy with her, she would have asked him to autograph it. She had never met anyone famous before, although, she had once seen Paul Newman and Joanne Woodward walking through O'Hare with "obvious friends, not bodyguards."

Although he knew there was no need to say it, Elihu couldn't stop himself from commenting—not for the first time—that maybe he used to be famous but he no longer was, and he was a good deal happier this way. He said, "a good deal happier," but as he said it, he was thinking he might have been happier these days, but he was country miles from being blissfully—not even close to more-than-moderately—happy.

Later that night over dinner at Café Florian, the kind of restaurant where the proprietors are glad to cater to university types, he did gauge that his generally unmoving happiness meter was inching higher. He attributed the change to Emily. It was not just because she was pretty, though not beautiful, with the seductive mouth and alive eyes and auburn hair that, loose tonight, fell to her shoulders, not just because what she was wearing was a simple wool sweater and pleated skirt with a big pin piercing it, a style he thought had long since faded. It was none of that. Maybe *some* of that. It was that she was an elusive blend of sophistication and naiveté.

He had never met anyone like her. There was something about her of the high school girl. Every once in a while she giggled, and when she did, placed both of her delicate hands over her mouth. But just when Elihu would determine that's who she was, and that who she was was definitely not for him, she would abruptly abandon those qualities. Instead, she would look him in the eye and call him on something he'd said.

He was about to pour more of the acceptable Florian wine into her glass when she covered the glass with her hand, looked him in the eye and said, "What was all that about no longer being famous?"

"I'm not famous," Elihu responded. "I *was* famous, and now I'm not."

"If you're not famous," Emily pressed, "why did I recognize you? How do I know so much about you? Why did Jennifer say she would have asked for your autograph? That doesn't happen to the average man in the street."

Elihu said, showily raveling spaghetti on his spoon, "I was famous—'public like a frog,' in Emily Dickinson's brilliant phrase—and now I'm no more and no less than your average man in the street."

"If you say so," Emily said.

"I do say so," Elihu said, and the subject was dropped.

It did not come up again in the six months they were together—mid-October to mid-May, actually the week Emily was taking her senior-year exams.

They were together mostly where he was renting. It was the second floor of a Victorian home—turret included—on South Blackstone Avenue within walking distance of the campus as well as near the necessary bookstores: Powell's and O'Gara & Wilson Limited on nearby East Fifty-Seventh Street. He had found the perfectly acceptable place on an administrative-building bulletin board to which he'd been directed by a student he had stopped the day he arrived. He had figured students were the ones to ask, as, packed-light suitcase in hand, he was casing the large, intellectual University of Chicago urban oasis.

The furnished second-floor, two-bedroom apartment suited him, although Mrs. Frances Brady, a large, buxom woman of innumerable housedresses who owned the house, looked as if she could turn out to be more of a busybody than he might have liked, especially if she ever found out he had once been not just Mr. Elihu Goulding but *the* Elihu Goulding. When she asked about him at their initial meeting, who he was and what he did (but didn't ask for references), he decided to say he was a lawyer disillusioned with the law and was thinking about becoming a teacher. He thought he'd try going back to school to see if he liked it.

The first time Emily came to the apartment with him—she was going to make dinner for them as a thank-you for the three or four meals out—Mrs. Brady just happened to be occupying the porch as they passed by on the short way to Elihu's separate entrance. Elihu introduced Emily to Mrs. Brady as a classmate. "Pleased to meet you, dear," Mrs. Brady said, and then, as Emily preceded him up the outside staircase to his door, the all-knowing-all-seeing landlady gave Elihu an exaggerated wink. He realized he should have known he was far from the first randy University of Chicago boarder Mrs. Brady had ever had under her gabled Victorian roof.

As Mrs. Brady got used to seeing Emily entering and exiting the apartment, with or without Elihu, and never did more than repeat the broad wink, Elihu also got used to Emily's comfortingly domestic comings and goings.

He was infatuated with her, and as far as he could tell, she was infatuated with him. He wasn't in love with her, he didn't think—or repeatedly told himself—nor was she with him, he assumed. For him, it was the naiveté alternating, sometimes within seconds, with the sophistication, that tickled him. For her, as she said every once in a while, he was a welcome break from the college boys she usually dated, all of them full of themselves and, as she put it, "predictably callow as hell. What is it with them?"

She was quick to admit she was young and in some things impressionable, but not, she reiterated, where relationships figured in. Despite her youth, she also was able to put Elihu's attentions in perspective. Perhaps the fittest words for their time together were ones she chose, not that they were in any way arcane.

For her it was "a senior-year University of Chicago fling." She regaled him with details of friends having the same experiences. He even met some of them and their swains, though Emily maintained some of what she saw as flings were regarded by their participants as preliminaries to marriage—"I suspect first marriages," she specified, the sophistication kicking in.

She was "damned" if she was going to marry straight out of college, which was one reason, she made plain to Elihu, that, as an older man with his often announced disregard for marriage, he was a lover—a lover preferable to other options she had—but decidedly "not husband material." (When was Elihu ever "husband material," he again questioned himself with satisfaction?) Although he often demurred when she said those things, he knew she was right. Every time she said anything about it—often just after they had made love and had uncommittedly hurled the word "love" around—he had to stop himself from openly sighing with relief.

Elihu's supposed belief in her conviction on the lovey-dovey matter, which did nothing to minimize their increasing sexual ardor (quite the opposite), was such that, when—during the first week of May and over a meal at Café Florian where they'd become regulars—Emily informed him with temperate measure that she was pregnant, his immediate reaction might have been manly composure. It wasn't. It was quiet panic.

Emily was ready for it. She let no time elapse before adding, "Not to worry. I don't expect you to marry me. You know I'm not ready to get married. On the other hand, and funny as it sounds, I think I *am* ready to be a mother."

"But-but-but," Elihu stammered, "I thought you were on the pill. You said you were on the pill."

"I was on the pill," Emily replied. "I went off it. I didn't tell you because it's my decision. You're not part of it."

Sometimes, Elihu thought to himself, there's such a thing as too much sophistication, too much precocity. He said, "but it's my child." He heard himself and added, "Too."

"But not a child I expect you to raise," Emily said. "I know you, Eli, and if I think I'm ready to be a mother, I don't think you're ready to be a father. I wouldn't bet you ever will be." How true that was, Elihu thought but kept his lip zipped. He did have an oddly vagrant thought. He thought of Jean. He thought of the miscarriage. Might that happen to Emily? He realized how illogical he was being. Out of sheer alarm. He banished the thought. Wherever it came from.

Emily said, "You're not saying anything. I can assume I'm right about your preferences?"

"But, Emily," Elihu said and pulled one of Emily's delicate hands to his chest, "there are obligations." Here he was making more sense.

"There aren't. I don't want money from you. I don't expect you to be around. You're only obligated to not say anything about whether I thought about an abortion. I didn't, and I won't. You know I'm not pro-life. I'm pro-choice, and I've made mine. I know this will sound crude, but if it helps, you can regard yourself as a friendly sperm donor."

"'A friendly sperm donor,'" Elihu said and chewed over the words. "I'm reduced to that."

"You're the man who wrote *Wandering Youth*, *For My Betters* and *The Accidental Immigrants*," Emily said and laughed the laugh Elihu had come to wait for. "In your case I don't think 'reduced' applies."

"Are you saying—?" Elihu started to ask, but Emily interrupted him.

"I'm not saying what you're about to ask," she said. "I haven't been waiting around to find the best biological father for a child I've been planning for a long time. I didn't spot you at Saul Bellow's lectures and think, 'Whoa, there's a guy who wrote novels that got him on the cover of *Time*. Maybe I should lay a trap for him.' I won't deny I figured you a likelier prospect than frat-boy Joe or the corner grocer. I have run across corner grocers that are stronger in certain male departments than you are. No frat boys, though. Now you know, and we can talk more about it later. Right now, finish your spaghetti and meatballs before they get cold."

Elihu and Emily did resume the discussion. It continued for the next few weeks. More than once, he offered to marry her. Trying to be offhand about it, he even used the cliché "make an honest woman of you." But Emily knew he didn't mean the proposal. What's more he knew she knew he knew he didn't mean the proposal. One night she opened her *For My Betters* copy and read him a passage where Sabe Levensohn says to his girlfriend, Essie Cohen, "All you talk about is marriage. Can't you get it into your admittedly good-looking head that I'm not the marrying type? I'm a post-bar-mitzvah boy, a Jew free to sow my wild kasha. I'll always be a post-bar-mitzvah boy. No choice about that. I'll always be a Jew. No choice about that. But I can choose to keep sowing my wild kasha, and the only way I know how to do that is by not marrying anyone, anytime, ever."

When she finished reading, she poked at the excerpt she'd just read with her slim right forefinger. He could have brushed the quote aside, but if he had, he would be lying, and Emily knew that as well. She poked the paragraph three times for emphasis.

He didn't press the point. As an alternative, he brought up the need he felt to help support the child. He reiterated his finances and compared them with her current circumstances—and those of her parents, whom he had never met but understood to be well enough off, as the parents of many, if not most, University of Chicago undergraduates are. He wagered that as an unmarried man with few obligations, including the one she wouldn't grant him, he was in a better position than the mother and father she'd told about her present status and who, also as enlightened University of Chicago parents customarily are, accepted her decision and insisted they would back her in it. What was not said to Elihu was the parents' dissatisfaction with her marrying a forty-two-year-old Jew, no matter how many Dewey decimal numbers he has to his credit. That wasn't said to him, but he would have wagered that it was said among themselves and their friends.

The month of May ended, and Elihu and Emily determined they'd go their separate ways, she to her Canton, Ohio, home to await the baby and think about the possibility of graduate school, he to wherever dictated by the figurative pin jabbed blindly in the figurative map. Yes, the month of May, fraught with all sorts of busy-ness, ended, but not before Emily okayed his insistence on sending a check maybe monthly, maybe only occasionally "if that makes you more comfortable, Emily." She promised to keep him posted on her whereabouts but said she didn't need to, or want to, keep tabs on his. She could look at the return addresses on envelopes. That's if he bothered to write the return addresses. Otherwise, they would just accept that after "a meaningful fling" they would part, likely forever. They wouldn't pretend it hadn't been meaningful, hadn't been valuable for them both in some of the same and some immensely different ways.

The parting took place on the sidewalk outside Emily's apartment, where roommates Joyce and Jennifer, both staying for another few weeks, stood aside when the cab Emily had called pulled up. So polite, so thoughtful of them. They knew, as good roommates do, that Emily and Elihu wanted to have a minute or two to themselves.

"Do you think you would ever write about this?" Emily asked while Elihu's arms were still around her.

"You and Saul Bellow know I don't write anymore," Elihu said. "So no, I won't write about it. It's ours alone."

They disengaged, and Elihu, Joyce and Jennifer saw Emily into the cab. Just before it pulled away, Emily stuck her right hand out of the open back window for him to hold one last time. It occurred to Elihu that he might kiss it, but they were saying farewell. Elihu did not figure this as the right time to play the gallant. Emily withdrew the hand, and with her left hand she patted her stomach. "I promise I'll keep you posted," she said.

Elihu watched the cab move away and thought that no, he wouldn't write about any of this, but he also thought that Emily could be a winning character in anyone's book. At twenty-two she remained unlike any young woman he had ever known. She knew what she wanted, but more significantly she knew what she didn't want. Even more cogent for him, she knew what he wanted and didn't want. She knew what he could stand, could take in, could take on. A twenty-two-year-old who still hadn't outgrown the giggles, she saw him for who he was—saw through him?—and it was that understanding that enabled them both to have this brief, now never to be sullied, moment.

Elihu left Chicago the next day for, it turned out, almost two years in Paris and living on Rue de Fleurus the entire time, just down the gently curving block from where Gertrude Stein and Alice B. Toklas entertained Pablo Picasso, Henri Matisse, Georges Braque and Guillaume Apollinaire as well as several sycophantic members of the lost generation. The proximity was the impetus for Elihu's devoting several months to reading Stein—but never to trying Toklas's recipes.

His first January there he dropped into American Express to retrieve his mail. Not caring much about mail one way or the other, he only stopped in once or twice a month. That rainy grey January day, he opened a blue envelope containing the birth announcement (November 5, 1993) of Ethan Gideon Haas. A photograph of an infant boy looking, as Elihu believed all infants looked, like Winston Churchill after having just lighted and drawn on a stale cigar.

"I have a son," Elihu murmured under his breath as he left the American Express office and looked over at the undulant side of the Garnier Opera House. "No. I don't have a son."

X.

Ethan finishes the breakfast Elihu prepared for him. The boy pulls away the napkin he'd tucked into his open collar and brusquely wipes his mouth with it.

Ethan looks at Elihu with a faint smile. Elihu knows the smile as a version of his own. Ethan says, "I guess I was hungry."

"When did you eat last?" Elihu asks.

"Oh, I had enough to eat recently enough," Ethan says. He sets his arms before him flat on the table. He's holding the crumpled napkin in the stubby fingers of his left hand.

Elihu knows nothing about Ethan yet, but he knows when young men are being vague so as not to embarrass themselves. He was one of them once. So was Seth Levy. So was Sabe Levensohn. He knows about saying anything necessary to get around admitting you need something from someone you can't get for yourself. You don't want to come across as weak, as unmanly.

"Do you have any money?" Elihu asks. "Do you need any?" He asks but he makes no move for his wallet.

"Do you think I came here looking for money?" Ethan says, tightening his left hand around the napkin and making a fist of his right hand. His expression tightens, too, the full lips clenching.

Elihu sees defiance in the eyes that so closely match his. "I have no idea why you came," Elihu says. He deliberately makes no change in the tone of his voice. "Maybe you want to tell me. If you know."

That seems to catch Ethan off guard. His hands relax. So does his expression. He appears to be thinking it over. Elihu waits with what he hopes is a neutral look.

"That's a good question, sir," Ethan says. "I guess I'm here because I want to know who my father is. My biological father. I know I don't have an honest-to-God father."

Elihu hears the "I guess." It's the second one in less than a minute. He recognizes that as another instance of a young man being reluctant to commit to something, to anything. "Is that what your mother told you," Elihu says, "that you have no father? You still haven't told me if your mother knows where you are."

"She doesn't know for sure," Ethan says, "but I think she has a pretty good idea."

"Oh, yes? And why is that?"

"You don't know my mom," Ethan says. He sets the napkin on the table and brings the bent left forefinger of his left hand to his mouth as if belatedly to stop what he had just said. It crosses Elihu's mind that Ethan is left-handed. Like Elihu. He looks at Ethan's right wrist, and sure enough he wears his watch there. Ethan, Elihu thinks, takes after me in that respect. For a split second something resembling pride pulses through Elihu. It's as if an atom broke free and hurtled on a new trajectory.

"I guess you do know my mom," Ethan says. "Or did."

"Don't you think you ought to call her to let her know where you are?"

"Probably, but not right now."

Elihu doesn't press it.

"But you don't know her now," Ethan goes on. "See, she never talks about you. She always finds a way to weasel out of talking about a dad when I start asking about him. About *you*. But a few weeks ago, I found a letter from—I guess it's your lawyers. She's kept them to herself, hidden them all these years, but somehow she missed this one. I found it and opened it and found the check your bank sent."

Ethan's mouth tightened again, not as firmly. Elihu thought that he—and Emily as well—recognized guilt on Ethan's Elihu-like face. "I mean, I didn't go looking for it. She left it lying around. I showed it to her and said, 'What's this?' She was mad as hell, but she told me. She said, 'You're old enough to know now.'"

All the time Ethan is saying this, he's looking around the room. He only looks directly at Elihu once or twice. Now he looks at Elihu. "She tells me about you. She's always said my biological father was a nice man, but she would never say any more. This time, she tells me it's you. It's this famous writer she had an affair with—'a loving affair,' she said—when she was young and not ready to be married. 'Loving' is the word she used. She said you may be my biological father, but you weren't ready to be my day-to-day father. She understood that. She told me about meeting you in Chicago and about your books. I'd seen them on her bookshelves. I'm not much of a reader. Of fiction. But I took your first book down and read it. Not bad. I really liked the part when Seth Levy goes out with Eileen Horgan from the other side of the tracks and what her Catholic father says to him when he goes to pick her up. A shitty thing to say. That even happened to me once. Something like it, anyway. My mom also made me promise I wouldn't try to contact you. I did. I promised. I made the promise."

"But you didn't keep it," Elihu says.

"I guess not." Ethan's eyes are wandering around the room.

"No need to guess," Elihu says. "You're sitting right here. You broke the promise. How did that come about?"

"Because it's not fair to ask a guy to make that kind of a promise about something so important," Ethan says, engaging Elihu again. "Don't you think getting to know who your father is—your biological father—is a natural thing to want to know?"

He doesn't wait for Elihu to respond. Elihu figures it's because Ethan believes he's asked a rhetorical question, if he actually knows what a rhetorical question is. He must. What little Elihu has picked up about Ethan hasn't yet led him to make that kind of assumption, to make any kind of assumption. Okay, Yale accepted him. Emily's lawyers had filled him in on that. So the boy can't be completely at sea. Sure, Ethan knows what a rhetorical question is. I can give him that much, Elihu silently concedes.

"Now that I knew that much about you," Ethan continues, "I wanted to know more. Not just the books. I saw the lawyers' address on the envelope. I googled them and got their number. How come the people you have handling your money are in Milwaukee?"

Again Ethan doesn't wait for a response. This time he isn't posing a rhetorical question. It's a real question, but he's unburdening himself and, it's obvious, doesn't want to stop for an answer. "I called them up and got a receptionist. I said I was calling for Mrs. Emily Haas, who received regular checks from an office client, and Mrs. Haas wanted to contact the client but had misplaced his address. The receptionist put me through to someone who right away gave me this address."

Ethan throws his arms up and says, "So here I am."

Elihu gets the impression that Ethan is trying to sound off-hand about his prowess but can't quite rise to that level. Nonchalance does not seem a typical trait in the young man's repertoire. Indeed, in Elihu's estimation, nonchalance is a quality that seems to have disappeared entirely from contemporary human discourse.

"Here you are," Elihu says. "Today. You're here now. You have met me. We've met. Where do you expect to go next? Home? Emily—your mother—is in Cleveland now, isn't she? Are you headed back there?" He pictures Ethan's luggage sitting by the front door and thinks there is more there than someone like Ethan would pack for a short trip. "Or are you on the road?" He puts the final three words in air quotes.

Ethan changes several expressions so fast that Elihu thinks he's watching a flipbook. "I thought I might stay here for a while," Ethan says and repeats some of the just-run expressions. Elihu thinks he discerns uncertainty, hope, anger, disbelief, disgust and more in the seconds they both sit without saying anything.

"Is this house yours?" Ethan asks. "I mean, do you own it? Do you rent it? Does anyone else live here? I mean, are there separate apartments or anything?"

"I have the whole house," Elihu says, "I'm renting it. I took a year's lease I can break anytime I want. Not that you need to know."

"So this is all yours," Ethan says. Now on the face Elihu knows from the mirror, he sees a modicum of assurance settle. "So you must have plenty of spare space. I wouldn't take up much of it. Maybe for one night, anyway. I don't know where else to go. I've never been in New York City before. I suppose I could try to find out if there are any youth hostels around. Do you know of any?"

Elihu looks at Ethan. He looks at this twenty-one-going-on-twenty-two-year-old. He thinks, This is my son. I am not a father, but this is my son. I do not see how I can turn him out. One night. I have room. But it's room I need for myself. How is this kid going to react to Handel being piped day and night upstairs and down?

He says, "Just the one night." Even as he says it with a noticeable chill in his voice, something tells him the one-night agreement will never hold.

xi.

The first decision Elihu must make, as he and the boy leave the kitchen, is where to bivouac Ethan. Why "bivouac" pierces his brain, he couldn't say. Maybe he can. The duffel bag, the forced-march soldier image Ethan conjures.

He settles on the second-floor front bedroom. Better Ethan should be the one putting up with street noise than he should. Elihu will occupy the second-floor back bedroom. It's only for a night.

That's should Elihu definitely choose to sleep in the back bedroom and not on one of the third-floor convertible beds. Hold on. Is he going to have to alter his loose routine to give this boy a sense of someone who sleeps in the same bed every night? Like conventional people? Like your everyday biological father?

Elihu doesn't have the answer to that question. What he has is that he's suddenly aware of thinking about altering his routine to accommodate someone else. Not just any someone else. He's about to accommodate a son.

He shoves the thought aside as he picks up the backpack Ethan had shed, leads the boy upstairs, pointing out the bathroom at the top—and where towels and bedding are stored. Damned if he's going to make up the bed, to change the sheets already there and fresh since Mrs. Woolard last changed them. Reaching the bedroom, he says, "This is it. I hope you like it."

Ethan says, "I like it. I'd like anything after some of the places I've crashed the last few nights."

Not the most grateful response, Elihu thinks, but keeps the thought to himself. Boys these days don't lend much credence to being grateful. Did they ever? Did he at Ethan's age? He realizes he has just compared himself to his son. He is resistant to acknowledging this is a father's reaction. He says, "I'll leave you alone to make yourself comfortable." He hears himself on the verge of having said "Make yourself at home." He buries the sentiment. It's something he might have said to any other guest—not that in his long-standing frame of mind he's prepared to have guests—but not to this one, for whom "home" could, very possibly would, have an entirely different meaning. This is *not* Ethan's home. This is not Ethan's home.

Elihu starts to leave the room but a somewhat questioning "Oh" from behind reaches him. He turns back. Ethan has put his suitcase and duffel bag down and is stepping a few feet forward towards the bedroom door where Elihu has stopped in his uncertain tracks.

Ethan says, "What do I call you? I don't know what to call you. I don't think I ought to call you Dad. I'm not ready for that." An all but discernible pleased look crosses Ethan's face. It's one Elihu had not yet seen. "I bet you're not ready for it, either," Ethan says and waits for the response.

Maybe I should have been ready for this, Elihu thinks, but he isn't. He thinks fast, because he knows he has to act fast. He says and musters a smile to accompany it, "Call me Elihu."

"Elihu," Ethan says, not mirroring the smile. "When my mother finally told me about you, she called you Eli."

That nonplusses Elihu. He hears the past couched in the remark, the tense indicating that Emily only talked about him the one time. Otherwise Ethan would have said, "My mother *calls* you Eli." Wouldn't he have?

"Anyway," Ethan says, "thanks, Elihu. Thanks for taking me in." As he goes back to his belongings, he adds, "I know you didn't have to."

Or did I have to, Elihu asks himself as he climbs the stairs to the library-study, where he intends to carry on doing whatever he feels like doing—resuming rereading *Tristram Shandy*, perhaps—as if nothing out of the ordinary has happened. *Is* happening. Yes, of course, I had to take the boy in, he informs himself. I couldn't turn him away like a mustachio-twirling villain in a nineteenth-century melodrama.

Elihu imagines himself in swirling cape, pointing and saying, "And never darken my doorstep again." He laughs coldly. He sits down in the green club chair and looks out at the garden where no early sign of spring is awakening the branches of the one tree. The oak? The chestnut? Nothing is blooming. I ought to do something with the garden, he tells himself. Since he's taken temporary ownership. he has only gone into it for three short turns—and then giving little more than cursory glances at the brown and grey surroundings.

When he has gone into the downstairs storage area, he has noticed garden tools and a pair of soiled gloves. Someone(s?) used them, he thought then and thinks again. He wonders if Ethan has any gardening skills. If so, the boy could earn whatever keep he's going to accumulate by working in the garden. From the look of things, Ethan doesn't have green thumbs (he does have Elihu's stubby thumbs), but Elihu warns himself not to abide too rigidly by the look of things.

He picks up *Tristram Shandy* and tries to reinsert himself into it. He cannot at first, his concerns veering to Ethan. Then he does and becomes so absorbed in Laurence Sterne's intrepid story that when he jolts out of it, he has to do what he frequently does when he gets lost reading.

He has to readjust himself. He rises, shakes his arms, his shoulders, as if he's just completed an exercise regimen. In a manner of speaking he has. Having done that, he looks at the garden. It's late afternoon. He can tell by the light. That's the best he can do. He has no clock in the library-study. Since he is on no fixed schedule, he has no need to keep close track of the time.

The only clock at 73 East Ninth Street is in the kitchen, where he has also allowed the only telephone. He's made a habit of minimizing distractions. He refuses to own a cell phone.

He puts *Tristram Shandy* back on top of the stack he keeps by the chair and by the hemp magazine holder, rubs his eyes, thinking fuzzily about Sterne's fractured father-son theme. How suddenly pertinent it is, damn it.

Ethan is downstairs. Should he check on the boy? Usually, Elihu avoids the word—the concept of—"should." He's made a decades-long habit of not doing anything because he feels he *should* do it. More like the polar opposite. Yet he's just invoked a "should" and decides he'll act on it.

Leaving the room to go downstairs, his legs suddenly feel heavy. Too much sedentary reading, he decides, intending to do nothing about it.

At Ethan's room—no, not Ethan's room, the second-floor front bedroom—he knocks lightly on the closed door. No response. He knocks again and again lightly. Again no response.

He opens the door slowly only several inches, enough to see the bed. Ethan is asleep on it. Ethan is sleeping on his right side. It strikes Elihu that he, too, sleeps on his right side. The boy has taken off his outer clothes. He is sleeping in a white T-shirt hitched up to expose his belly. He's in boxer shorts with the fly slightly askew. He has removed his boots but not the bulky Army socks. His legs are splayed. His thighs are thick, his calves are thick. My legs, Elihu thinks, are just as hairy. Ethan's left arm is flung over the edge of the bed. His right arm is under the pillow he appears to be clutching. He has pulled the pillow from under the chenille bedspread.

Elihu always thought there was something comical about chenille, maybe because Jean and her friends thought chenille was elegant. Probably the word itself lent it that cachet, the Frenchness of it.

Ethan has not bothered to get under the chenille and the white top sheet. His mouth is slightly open, and from where Elihu stands he hears a muffled snore. The aroma wafting his way remains evidence of Ethan's unwashed traveling time. When Ethan wakes up, Elihu may have to suggest a shower.

Elihu continues to watch for a minute or more, thinking his presence might cause Ethan to awake. Or shift his position. Or do something to indicate he is dreaming. Other than his right thumb moving in a swift jerk, nothing of the sort takes place.

Elihu thinks something he is alarmed to discover he's thinking, to discover he's taking in. I am watching my son sleep. My son is sleeping not ten feet from me. I have a son, and I'm watching him sleep. I've had a son for over twenty years, and now I'm watching him sleep. I never saw him sleep as fathers, as parents, do from a boy's infancy on. I haven't done that. I'm catching up now. This is what it's like.

I'm doing this belated catching up, this meager catching up. The thought causes him to close the door and retreat. He thinks, I forfeited the right twenty-one years and some seven or eight months ago. ("Twenty-one going on twenty-two," indeed.) I forfeited the right, although I agreed to help support him. I agreed to send checks regularly. I insisted on it. It was the least I could do, and I wanted to do the least I could do. Emily only hesitantly allowed me to do that much. She made it clear, but even that trifling action could be interpreted as in some manner securing, as in some manner buying Ethan's—Ethan's what?—surely not his love, not his affection. But perhaps buying his appreciation? From a safe remove? His distant respect? His estranged fealty?

I've earned nothing, Elihu thinks, save the obligation to give him a day's hospitality—or perhaps several more days' hospitality, depending.

He has told me he doesn't think of me as a father to him, and although he is my biological son, there's more to fatherhood. I chose to forgo all that. I do not regret it. I am not his father in the meaningful sense. I am not his father in the real sense, in the substantive sense, in the realistically legitimate sense. I'm Elihu Goulding to him. He's Ethan Haas to me. That's all there is to it. All there is to it.

Elihu remembers something. Over the years Emily has sent him photographs of Ethan. Every couple of years, not more frequently. He estimates he has received at most ten, a dozen. When she sent the first couple, she cautiously let him know she expected nothing in return. He has never been certain how to take them. Has there been something wishful about them? Proud? Has she meant them as a rebuke? Was she rubbing it in, whatever "it" was in her mind? Has she meant them to be no more than a record?

Elihu afforded them little attention. Any more, he considered, might nudge something in him he did not want nudged. When he received them—when he fingered the envelopes in which Emily enclosed them—he knew what was inside. He took them from the envelope, glanced at them, put them aside. He never looked at them again but did not discard them. Discarding them, he reasoned to himself every time, was a form of blanking Ethan out, of denying his existence, of extinguishing him.

That, he wasn't able to do. Instead, after he had perused the first one (six-month-old, pudgy-faced Ethan in a bassinet waving arms and feet), he opened an old cigar box of his father's in which he'd saved a few—a very few—photographs, some of family members, some of random objects he'd used for research purposes. He dropped the first photograph in the box face down, not to be looked at again. Subsequently, whenever another materialized, he took a few seconds to take it in, as if scrutinizing clues to a mystery he did not care to solve. Then, unceremoniously, he added it to the cigar box collection.

He knows where the cigar box is. He always has it with him. He has placed it in one of the low cabinets in the library-study. He returns upstairs to retrieve it. He does and takes the cigar box to the club chair, sits down with it.

He opens it and sees the photographs, which are, he realizes, the only photographs he has put in since he received the first one. He takes them out, flips through them, counts them. There are only nine.

Because he has never perused them again—let alone examined them for epiphanies—the most recent is on top. He decides to examine them that way, which, he tells himself with a slight hint of wry amusement, is like rewinding the clock of Ethan's life. Giving himself a chuckle (is it a sneer?), he muses that yes, there are instances when you can reverse time—photographs are one instance and fiction—no question about it—another.

The one on top shows Ethan looking abashed in cap and gown. The cap's tassel is set so that it falls over his nose. It's like a joke, but is it a deliberate joke—Ethan's joke on himself? Or is it simply an awkward sartorial accident making Ethan look even goofier in an ill-fitting academic gown than, Elihu thinks, students generally do in graduation photographs? Ethan is standing in front of a brick building, presumably his Cleveland high school. It couldn't be Yale. Elihu had learned some time before, through Emily's law office, that Ethan had dropped out of Yale. He turns the photograph over and sees that Emily (he still recognizes her handwriting) has written the date: "Graduation, June 2013."

He puts the photograph aside, atop *Tristram Shandy*, and looks at the next one, which from Emily's notation on the back, was taken three years before the previous photograph. Ethan is in full-blown football uniform, holding a helmet. He played football, Elihu thinks, something I never did. He wonders how accomplished Ethan was at the sport. The affectless expression he wears is no tip-off. If there's any giveaway in Ethan's empty gaze, it's that he is (possibly?) annoyed at having to pose for the photograph.

In the next, that carries no date on the back (Elihu estimates it must again be from two or three years earlier), Ethan is standing astride a mountain bike. His sturdy right leg is stationed on a driveway that could or couldn't be the driveway where Emily and Ethan are living. The ranch house in the background seems to be the house next door. (He doesn't see Emily living in a ranch house. He sees her in someplace more traditional.) Ethan's left foot is on the left pedal. He's wearing a T-shirt that says "Metallica," khaki shorts riding high on his thighs and on his head a plastic helmet apparently molded to suggest Mercury winging along. It's evident that again he's posing for the camera but not necessarily enthusiastic about it. Nonetheless, he appears robust, well fed.

Ethan looks to be about twelve in the next photograph. He's lying heavily on a leather couch watching television. Or is he sleeping? It isn't clear. He's wearing pajamas dotted with footballs and goal posts, which might suggest he's fallen asleep. The implication is that, at the least, Emily had caught him off-guard. On the back she's written "Ethan melts into the couch during Super Bowl XLI."

Emily didn't take the next photograph. It's one of those schoolroom shots, where the student is seated at a desk, hands folded in front of him. Ethan, canted slightly right and looking just this side of bored, is wearing a white shirt, a tie tightly knotted and a solid-color V-neck sweater. It's a larger photograph with, in the lower left-hand corner, the words "Seymour Lipkin Photography." On the back, Emily has written "Ethan, 10. Sixth grade. His teacher, Miss O'Donnell, says he has 'a workable aptitude,'" whatever that's intended to indicate.

It doesn't appear as if Emily is responsible for the next photograph, either. Elihu can't be certain that she isn't in it, at least part of her. Ethan is sitting on a sofa, looking to his left questioningly. There is a hand on his right shoulder, a woman's hand. To his left is only part of the figure to whom the hand belongs. Ethan is dressed in a blazer and trousers. The woman—Elihu assumes it must be Emily—is wearing a wool suit. Behind them is striped wallpaper, and above them the lower section of a wide mirror reflecting nothing that Elihu can discern. From the looks of a certain kind of formality, he imagines Emily and Ethan are visiting friends, maybe relatives (Emily's family?) on a special occasion. Perhaps whoever snapped the photograph is someone wanting a record of the event and has determined that everyone present must be accounted for. Maybe only Ethan and part of Emily have been honored. But why, if it is Emily, why isn't she photographed in full? Is it she? If so, did she, knowing she would send a copy of the photograph to Elihu, ask not to be shown? Perhaps everyone present was photographed separately and, predictably, Emily chose not to send a picture of herself. And why is Ethan looking at the woman's hand as if disturbed that it's there proprietarily? On the back, Emily has written, "At the Shapiros with my best escort." Who are the Shapiros? There's a date, but it's smudged.

Next, Ethan blowing out candles on a birthday cake. This one is interesting to Elihu for cues that might be noticeable to anyone looking at it but certainly shouldn't be quickly dismissed—as he must have dismissed it when it first arrived—by anyone writing fiction and habitually looking to register giveaway details for potential future fictional purposes. On the decorated table in the photograph there's a tiny dunce cap with an elastic chin band. It's not on Ethan's head. It's lying several inches from him and from the birthday cake, as if it's either not been put on for the big moment or has already been snatched off and pushed aside. If Emily took this picture, she was standing far enough from Ethan to include a view of three or four feet to the boy's right and left and a few more feet behind where there's a right-of-center glimpse into a well-lighted kitchen. That's to say that the photograph would have included, Elihu thinks, at least some party guests surrounding Ethan, were any present. None are visible. What? No party guests? On the back of the photograph Emily wrote "Ethan is five."

In the next photograph Ethan in full body profile rides a tricycle. Because the photograph is slightly blurry, he must have been pedaling quickly along the pavement of what looks to be a standard suburban neighborhood, probably Emily's and Ethan's Cleveland neighborhood. Or maybe Canton, were Emily still living there. (He's never kept close track of her return addresses.) Although Elihu can't be certain, it looks as if Ethan's right leg is soiled or bruised. Either possibility suggests the standard hallmarks of an active (hyperactive?) boy. He knows that boys presenting such physical affects would have been considered Ritalin candidates at any time in the past several decades. He wonders if the overused A.D.D, or A.D.H.D. diagnosis has ever been pinned on Ethan. He hopes not. He suspects Emily wouldn't fall for that. On the back of the photograph she had written "My 3-year-old speed king in Oshkosh overalls." Recalling Emily's disdain for brand-name status symbols, Elihu knows the Oshkosh reference is her aiming an old in-joke at him.

The last and first photograph is the one of Ethan waving his plump arms and legs—an infant still at the age when grabbing a foot is an instinctive affair, intuitive calisthenics. He imagines the sleeping Ethan he just looked in on suddenly waking up and impulsively reaching out an arm to lift a socked foot. The Ethan in the photograph has a round face not unlike most infants at that age. He turns the photograph over. Emily has written, "Ethan at six months—a solemn baby. Not unlike you. Okay, not the 'baby' part." Elihu objects to being characterized as solemn. He doesn't remember himself as being solemn when he was with Emily.

Not all the time. He thought she had brought out a certain joviality in him. But maybe the joviality he thought she brought out in him wasn't sufficiently jovial to correspond with her definition of joviality. They had often found things to laugh about, hadn't they? He knows they had. He isn't making it up. Maybe she was just exaggerating his solemnity. He won't deny he had a tendency to be solemn. Look at him today.

Once Elihu has examined the final photograph of Ethan, he places it back in the cigar box as he has the others, image up. He picks them up again, scans them again, replaces them in reverse chronological order, sets the cigar box on the floor in front of him. In a manner of speaking he has done something else he never thought of doing once he and Emily parted. He has watched Ethan grow up.

He corrects himself. He has done nothing of the sort. He's looked at nine photographs. That's it. That's all. He knows nothing about Ethan's growing up. Nothing. He has the urge to list the things he does not know, the endless things. He thinks of his not watching Ethan take his first steps, of Ethan left off for his first day of kindergarten. What kind of father is he? No kind of father. Elihu stops there. He wants to imagine nothing more. What would be the point? Twenty years and some months earlier he removed himself from all that. Just because a boy shows up on his doorstep a few hours earlier, he has no reason to change his mind.

He hears a throat being cleared behind him, a baritone throat-clearing. He turns slightly but not enough to see Ethan. "I don't want to interrupt you," Ethan says, "but I—."

Elihu stands up to emphasize his saying, "You're not interrupting me." He notices the cigar box lying at his feet. He feels he's been caught doing something he should not have been doing, as if, he has to chuckle to himself, he has been caught scratching his crotch. He realizes that from where Ethan is standing he can't see the cigar box. Even if he could, he knows nothing of its contents.

Now facing Ethan full on, Elihu continues. "I finished what I was doing. More or less. What about you? Did you sleep well?"

"I sure did," Ethan says. "I needed it." He's standing in the clothes he had on while he slept. He's a presence. He's a specter. Elihu knows it's Ethan standing there, but he still has to convince himself to take the boy in as real, as someone quite distinct from a manifestation of himself at that age. "How long did I sleep? Musta been a couple hours. I lost track. Nice bed, though."

Elihu says, "I'm glad you like it. Have you had a shower? You might want to."

"Yeah, I could use a shower," Ethan says. He raises his left arm and reflexively sniffs his armpit where there's a distorted oval of dried sweat. Ethan takes on an abashed look. "I probably should of showered before I took that nap."

Elihu realizes his asking could have sounded like an accusation. Wanting to disabuse Ethan of that, he says, "There's no should or shouldn't about it. I just thought you might not have had too many chances to shower. On your trip. If you want to now, go ahead. When you're done, we can go somewhere for dinner. You can tell me more about yourself." As an afterthought, he adds, "And your mother."

"There isn't that much more to tell," Ethan says. He starts to the door. "But dinner sounds good." He stops at the door. "I don't want to put you out."

"You're not putting me out," Elihu says.

"Oh, okay," Ethan says and leaves. "As long as I'm not putting you out."

Elihu wonders if he just detected a hint of sarcasm in the remark. No, it must be his imagination, imagination informed by his own cynicism.

He hears Ethan's socked feet receding. He wants to think about what's happening. He doesn't know what to think.

Elihu thinks that if he's going out to eat—if he's going to take Ethan out to eat—he had better change his clothes. Is that what fathers do when taking a grown son out for a meal? Maybe it isn't what's customarily done these days. Not that he accepts he's a father in any more than the most literal terms. He is still standing by the club chair. He hears the forthright Concerti Grossi strains on the loop he's established. Since he first decided it was to be the background music for his life, such as his life at 73 East Ninth Street would become, he has almost never stopped it. He has thought about changing to something else—Chopin, Schubert, Liszt— but in the handful of moments he contemplated a change, he has decided the *Concerti Grossi* continue to suit him. At the same time as the concerti are stately, which gives him a sense of rectitude, he appreciates them for an underlying propulsive anxiety they contain.

The concerti have become reassuring. That's when he even notices them. Much of the time he doesn't hear them. Not really. Over the weeks and months they have become white noise.

But just now and unexpectedly, he hears them acutely. He realizes he is hearing them through different ears. He is hearing them with Ethan's ears. More precisely, he is hearing them through Ethan's ears and therefore has no idea how they are heard.

They have been piped through the house ever since Ethan entered it, but what is Ethan making of them? If anything? One thing Elihu knows is that Ethan slept through them for four hours. He also knows that Ethan has not mentioned the uninterrupted music. Perhaps he likes it. Maybe Ethan likes Handel. That's possible. But in one of the photographs, Ethan is wearing a Metallica T-shirt. Is he, God forbid, a metal-rock fan? There's been no mention of that, either, but that's not to say at any minute Ethan could pull earphones out of his backpack. Hold on. If Elihu remembers correctly, the Metallica T-shirt was in the photo Ethan had on when he was about fifteen.

He sits down again, picks up the cigar box, opens it, sorts through the photographs, finds the one with Ethan on a bicycle. That's the one. Ethan looks fifteen, sixteen: the age for Metallica. Maybe by now he's outgrown the group and regards it as a phase he went through. That's if he actually liked them then or just had the T-shirt on for no particular reason, except maybe to impress his friends.

Maybe he still does like them but, no matter how long he might stay, won't mind listening to something else. Like what? Like Handel? Like something Elihu cannot abide? Wait a second. This is Elihu's home. He can listen to whatever he wants to listen to. More than that, he did not invite Ethan. Ethan arrived on his own and can damn well listen to whatever gets played, no matter if it is the same thing over and over.

Sitting in the chair, Elihu feels himself getting hot under the collar—or would be if he were wearing a shirt with a collar. He imagines that if he could see himself, he would be seeing himself red-faced. He looks at the window. The February light has faded. He sees himself reflected there. He does not appear to have a red face. He looks as he always does these days. He neither likes nor dislikes the man he sees, the father of the twenty-one-year-old downstairs getting ready to eat out.

He puts the photographs back in the cigar box by his preferred order, rises and returns the collection to the cabinet where it is currently being stored.

xii.

Elihu takes Ethan to Gene's on West Eleventh Street. It's one of the neighborhood restaurants where he has come to feel comfortable. A five-minute walk, if that, and then down three steps, it's not as dark as he likes, but there are compensations. The clientele is comprised of men and women in their later years, most, if not all, of whom look to live within the same radius he does. Some of them know others of them and stop to say hello to each other on the way in and out, but not to him if he asks to sit at one of the tables for two at the back. He faces the back wall where he can rely on being left on his own. The phrase commonly invoked in England—"He keeps himself to himself"—repeats in his head shortly after he takes his seat. Here as well as in any of the restaurants he's taken to frequenting. The waiters (there are no waitresses) are—it's a blessing—no more nor less than professionally friendly. The most they'll do is offer a minimal smile and suggest that one of the entrees he's now known to order is especially good that night.

There isn't much to say about the Gene's décor—other than that the tablecloths are immaculately white, and there is a long mirror and generic prints on the walls of the long dining area showing what look like different views of the Italian countryside. The food, including the preorder plate of carrots, celery and radishes, is more than serviceable. Italian-American cuisine is what it might be called if any of the neighbors ever bothered to call it anything.

Now he is at one of the tables for two and, as customarily, is facing the wall. He does not tell Ethan he prefers to sit facing the back but says instead that he will face that way so that Ethan may take in the room. Ethan does what he's told and when they had settled into their chairs, says about the chattering diners, "They're mostly old—older—aren't they?"

For dinner Ethan has changed his clothes. Having checked his parka at the front, he is wearing a shapeless maroon sweater and black trousers. The boots are the same and, Elihu thinks, reveal signs of the road. Ethan has shaved and combed his springy hair, which for the most part remains in place when he takes off his knitted black cap.

Elihu explains about the "simple but nourishing" food. Ethan listens. They order. Ethan opts for chicken parmigiana with a side of spaghetti. Elihu has never had the dish at Gene's but figures that's the kind of heavy-calorie meal a growing boy goes for. Then he thinks that Ethan is past growing-boy stage but doesn't look it.

Elihu orders sole meuniere for himself. When the waiter leaves, there are several seconds of silence. Needless to say, Elihu has no idea what Ethan is thinking. He knows what he himself is thinking. I'm sitting at Gene's facing a stranger who happens to be my son. What do I say to him? He says, "Tell me about your mother."

Ethan says, "She once said that if I ever met you, you probably wouldn't ask too much about her. She said if you did, I should say she's fine and leave it at that." He follows what he's just said with a smile Elihu has no way to interpret.

He wonders if he has ever had that smile on his own face. Has he ever caught it in a mirror? He doesn't recognize it. He says, "Is she?"

"Is she what?"

"Is she fine?"

"I guess so."

"You only guess?" Elihu is becoming annoyed at Ethan's guesses. If it keeps up, he may have to say something about them. Then again, it's not his place, is it? It might be a father's place, but not his. Maybe it's not even a father's place if the father is parent-savvy.

"I guess she's fine," Ethan says. "I think she's fine. Really fine."

"You haven't called her yet?"

"No, not yet. I think she's happy with Mitchell. Happier than she was with the previous one."

"Mitchell?" Elihu asks.

"Lombardo," Ethan says. "He's okay. Fred, uh, Frederick Cowles, the first one, wasn't so hot. Emily wasn't too eager for you to know about him. She'd be mad if she knew I mentioned him." He stops to see how Elihu is reacting and then continues. "But about five years ago she married Mitchell. He's an estate lawyer, whatever that really means. I didn't like him very much at first, but she does, and I guess he's all right. He didn't like me very much at first, either. He was probably right not to. I don't know how likable I was to him. I'd had so much grief with Fred. Emily says—."

Elihu cuts him off. "You call your mother Emily?"

"Why not? It's her name." This said with a tinge of vehemence that interests Elihu, but then Ethan relents with "The last few years I call her that anyway. She says she doesn't always understand me. She doesn't understand why I'm twenty-one and dropped out of college. In my junior year, no less. Oh, yeah, I think you know I got into your alma mater and tried to stick it out, but finally I dropped out. Too many phonies, for one thing."

"Phonies." Hearing the word, Elihu thinks of *The Catcher in the Rye*. Didn't Holden Caulfield make a habit of calling everyone a phony, setting off a widespread overuse of the word? Is Ethan a late adopter of the tiresome cliché that J. D. Salinger set in motion, perhaps having no idea what he was doing? Elihu hopes not.

Ethan is continuing. "Now Emily doesn't understand why I don't have a job. We never argue, you know. She says she's too fed up to argue. All the time Emily says—for years she says—if I had a father, *he* might understand me. *She* doesn't. Finally, two weeks ago, she said it again, which is one time too many. I tell her I have a father. She laughs and says, 'You don't know how to find him.' That's why I say she doesn't know where I am, but she does."

Elihu is listening to Ethan's unexpected torrent of words and cannot decide what to take in first. He is trying to reconcile the Emily Haas that Ethan is describing with the Emily Haas he knew. Has she kept her name? Maybe she did, so the monthly checks would reach her. He does not know her as a mother, he points out to himself. In his experience, people usually change when they become parents. That's as good a reason as any he can give himself for not wanting to become a parent. The very word gets under his thin skin.

Ethan is charging on. "You know, she made me read your books. Not really made me, but I could tell she wanted me to. That's really why I got the first one out and then the other two. After she told me who you were. Are."

"Who I no longer am," Elihu is compelled to say. "You said you read *Wandering Youth* and thought it was 'not bad,' if I remember correctly." There's more acid in his tone than he wishes were there. But the thought that he is father to a boy who has read his books—*Wandering Youth* about himself at the age Ethan is now—would never have occurred to him, had never occurred to him before this very day. The thought comes to him that had he known a boy to whom he was a father would read a book he had written, would he have written it differently?

Strike the crazy thought. Or is it so crazy? Deny that *Wandering Youth* is autobiographical fiction, as he might and did in the early days (*For My Betters* as well), that's patently what it was. What it is, much as he wouldn't mind disavowing it now to Ethan. Would he want a son of his, a son with any insight whatsoever, to have an extended glimpse at his own life as a young man?

"Yeah," Ethan is going on, "Emily thought that if I wouldn't ever know you, she said she was glad at least I would know Elihu Goulding, the erstwhile author. Who he was."

The "erstwhile" catches Elihu's ear. It doesn't seem to him a word that Ethan, little as he knows the boy, would use. "Is that how she described me? 'The *erstwhile* author'?"

"Just the one time."

This stops Elihu. "I wonder what she means by that."

Ethan says, "You know what 'erstwhile' means, don't you? Sometimes, like in the past. Once."

"Yes," Elihu says. "I know what 'erstwhile' means."

"She's right, isn't she?" Ethan goes on. "You don't write anymore, do you?" He looks closely at Elihu. "Do you? Are you writing something now?"

Elihu shakes his head. The food has arrived. Elihu is picking at it. Ethan is more aggressive. "I'm not writing anything now," Elihu says and somehow hears it as a tempered admission, implying no more than a temporary hiatus.

Between growing-boy bites, Ethan asks, "Are you about to?"

"Not so far as I know," Elihu says.

"Then Emily is right. You're an erstwhile author. She said you already were when the two of you met. She said she was always trying to get you to write, but you were convinced."

Elihu remembers that. He has not thought of Emily's cajoling since he left her, since they had left each other. At the time, he says to himself now as he had then, her frequent admonishments about his resuming writing—always couched in terms he knew she thought were subtle, kittenish and eventually dropped—was one of the reasons he felt less disturbed at the end of the affair.

"Too bad," Ethan says. "The books of yours I read—*For My Betters*, the other two, too—were pretty good, you know, not bad, some of the best I've read, but I'm not a good judge. I'm more into non-fiction."

He's read *Wandering Youth*, Elihu thinks. He's read *For My Betters*. He's read—God forbid—*The Accidental Immigrants*. Elihu does not know how to take any of this. First off, why does he care what this kid thinks of his books? He's not certain what *he* thinks of them. He always has them on the bookshelves wherever he happens to be. If there are bookshelves. Usually there are. When there haven't been, he sometimes has them built for the books or just keeps them boxed. But he has not reread them in years, not once since he found out Saul Bellow thought Elihu Goulding was "promising."

But now he's curious. He's tempted to find out in what way Ethan thought they were not bad. Giving in to the temptation he asks. "What did you like about them?"

"Like I said, I read *Wandering Youth*, and *For My Betters* and *The Accidental Immigrants*," Ethan said. "Those are the right titles, aren't they? And by the way, I liked *The Accidental Immigrants* the best of them."

Whoa, huh? Elihu thinks. How can it be? But what does this kid know? He could challenge Ethan on that one. He reins himself in, only saying, "You got the titles right. You said you liked the part in *Wandering Youth* about Seth Levy and Eileen Horgan. What else did you like about them?"

"I liked the main character Seth all the way through, and Sabe in *For My Betters*."

"Seth Levy and Sabe Levensohn. What did you like about them?"

"I could relate to them. I could relate to someone brought up back then. Brought up very Jewish, of course. I'm not very Jewish, even though

Emily is not Jewish but thought I should know something about it. Because you are."

"Jewish, yes. Practicing, no. When I was writing, I think that was my slant on Jews. Not in *The Accidental Immigrants*, of course."

"Yeah, that's what Emily says. At least you weren't very Jewish when she knew you."

"I'm less so now," Elihu says, which is true. "What about you, Ethan? How Jewish did you become? If at all. In your mind? Since your mother isn't Jewish. Since her parents, your grandparents on her side aren't."

"Weren't," Ethan interjects.

"Sorry to hear that. Weren't."

"But Emily brought me up to respect religions, all religions, even if I'm not religious myself."

Something hits Elihu. "You didn't have a bar mitzvah, did you?"

"Fuck no," Ethan says and then, "Sorry, but no, I didn't have a bar mitzvah, but I am circumcised."

Elihu has the thought that there is no bar mitzvah photograph among the nine Emily has sent. Surely, there would be had there been one. He imagines Ethan in yarmulke, tallit and tefillin, while knowing that even had Ethan had a bar mitzvah it wasn't likely to be either an orthodox or conservative ceremony. He thinks that neither Frederick Cowles nor Mitchell Lombardo, had either been around when Ethan turned thirteen, would have pressed for a bar mitzvah. Given their surnames. He also thinks that Ethan's possible circumcision isn't something to which he has ever given any consideration. To Elihu that information registers more as a non sequitur.

He is trying to formulate a bar mitzvah subject response, when a woman approaches the table, a plump woman in her sixties or seventies in a cardigan and flannel skirt. He recognizes her as one of the many Gene's regulars. "Excuse me," she says, "I don't mean to interrupt."

Elihu suppresses the urge to say, "Of course, you mean to interrupt or you wouldn't have." He stops himself as much for Ethan's sake as for his. Not for the woman's. For a reason he can't quite codify, he doesn't want Ethan to see him in an aggravated state. Instead he says in a calculatedly neutral tone, "That's all right."

"Oh," she says in a cultivated dulcet way, "Forgive me, but I've seen you here before, and forgive me if I'm wrong, but aren't you Elihu Goulding, the writer? I think I recognize you from a photograph on one of your books."

At any other time, Elihu would have denied outright his being Elihu Goulding the writer. He would have said that no, he wasn't the writer but that every once in a while he is mistaken for him, usually by readers. He would have also decided on the instant that Gene's has to be crossed off his list of reliable hideaways.

But he's with Ethan and doesn't want to lie about his identity in front of him. He isn't certain why. Perhaps to Ethan, he imagines, his denying he is Elihu Goulding might seem inexplicably petty. He doesn't want to go into the lengthy explanation it would require. He doesn't care to seem as if he is just any celebrity denying who he is simply to be left alone. There is more to it than that, more, as Elihu sees it, about which Ethan has no need to be alerted.

He says, "Yes, I am Elihu Goulding."

"I knew I recognized you from your photograph. Even though it was taken some time ago. I told my friend I was sure it was you." With that, she turns and points at another table for two where a thinner woman about the same age as the interloper is flaunting a supercilious grin. "I've said so for weeks. She said, 'Ginge, you're wrong.' That's me—Ginger

Hochman. She said, 'He disappeared long ago.' I said, 'Yes, Becky, he disappeared to Gene's where he's been coming with some regularity.' You must have seen us. We're here every Monday and Thursday, a regular thing. After our mahjong game. So you *are* Elihu Goulding?"

She waits for a second acknowledgment and gets it. "Yes, I am." Elihu hasn't had to deal with this sort of activity in so long he has to remember the retired "mistaken for him" ploy, but these are radically different circumstances having to do with his unexpected dinner companion. All he thinks to say is, "Thank you for introducing yourself, Ms. Hochman, and now if you don't mind I'd like to, we'd like to get back to—."

Ginge Hochman hasn't finished. "I just wanted to say how much I love your books. I've read *Wandering Youth* more than once. Three times, I think. And *For My Betters*. But I think my favorite is *The Accidental Immigrants*."

Another one, Elihu thinks. Is he being ganged up on?

"I just love it," Ginge Hochman says and puts small, crossed hands over her heart. "When I read it, I just felt you were writing about my grandparents and how they came to this country. I can tell you it made me cry. Oh, that last scene when Addie Kovar realizes that Isaac has died, and she'll have to make her way alone."

Elihu has never had a response like that on *The Accidental Immigrants*. Ethan's minutes earlier doesn't qualify. His instantaneous reaction is a dart of pleasure he instantaneously squelches. He has all but forgotten about Addie and Isaac Kovar, Isaac born Kovarski. Why should he remember them? He has given up writing. He doesn't want to think about it.

"If I remember to, next time I'm here I'll bring at least one of your books for you to sign," Ginge Hochman says, which strikes fear into Elihu. "I already have a signed copy of *For My Betters*. I got that when it first came out. You signed it at Scribner's. I don't know why I haven't insisted on getting my book club to read it. Or *Wandering Youth* or *The Accidental Immigrants*. I don't know why I haven't thought of it until now. I should, and then maybe you could come talk to us about them."

The fear struck into Elihu rises higher. He is baffled by it. It must be due to his not having had to entertain the possibility of discussing his writing, his books, for so long. He knows he will go nowhere near accommodating Ginge Hochman and her book club. Likely he'd be slotted to follow the give-and-take on Jane Austen's *Pride and Prejudice*? Or some such. He's unaccustomedly tongue-tied all the same.

"And this must be your son," Ginge Hochman forges on. "He has to be. He's the spitting image of you." She turns to Ethan and asks, "What's your name?"

Elihu has noticed Ethan taking in the Hochman exchange with an expression giving away nothing more than bland interest. Ethan says, "Ethan."

"Ethan," Ginge Hochman repeats. "Ethan Goulding. A good, sturdy name."

Elihu is moved to contradict her—to establish that Ethan is Ethan Haas—but knows that will only open the door to additional explanations. He lets it slide. So does Ethan, which allows Ginge Hochman to carry on.

"And do you want to be a writer, too? Like your father?" she inquires.

Ethan is thinking what to say to the question, but Elihu preempts him. "No, he doesn't," he says.

The severity with which he says it escapes Ginge Hochman. She says to Ethan. "Oh, you want to be a doctor or a lawyer. Reliable professions."

"No," Ethan says, "I don't want to be a doctor or a lawyer."

By now, Elihu has had enough. To Ginge Hochman he says, as if the butter Gene's serves in neat gold wrappers wouldn't melt in his mouth, "Thank you so much for saying hello, Ms. Hochman, but Ethan and I really need to get back to our food."

"Of course, you do," Ginge Hochman says. "You must excuse me for interrupting your meal. I've got to get back to Becky myself. But next time I see you, I'm going to have a book for you to sign. I promise." She made to go but then added, "Nice meeting you, too, Ethan Goulding. I bet whatever you decide to do with your life, you'll be as good at it as your father is at writing novels."

Ginge Hochman is gone at last. Elihu doesn't watch her return to Becky no-last-name-given at the table three tables away. He looks down at his plate to recall what entrée he had ordered.

Given what had just transpired, he figures his best approach is to behave as if nothing had transpired.

Ethan isn't ready to dismiss it. "What was that?" he asks. Elihu sees that Ethan is looking past him at the table where Ginge Hochman must now be seated with her back to them. "Does that happen a lot?"

Elihu has to answer. "It never happens."

"It just did."

"It used to happen when I was younger," Elihu responds. "It's one of the reasons I stopped writing. I didn't like turning myself over to the public the way successful authors are expected to." He gave that further thought. "That's the way I saw it."

Elihu is lying and knows he is. That's not why he stopped writing, but it makes a good story to tell the boy. He reminds himself that he stopped writing because he was not good enough. His first two books were strictly luck. He knocked them out because he knew the facts of his life and could get them down in notebooks with conveniently fudging changes here and there.

"Something like Ginge Hochman hasn't happened to me in years," he says. "I'll damn well see it doesn't happen again any time soon." He has already resolved he is never returning to Gene's. That'll do it for signing Ginge Hochman's copy of *The Accidental Immigrants*. And what if she leaks it to other Gene's habitués, and they start lining up with their copies?

"You mean you won't be drinking tea and eating cookies at her book club?" Ethan asks. Elihu finished snapping out "You bet I won't" before he realized that Ethan was joking. To his defense, this was the first joke—or semi-joke—Ethan had made since he'd gotten up from the stoop.

What do you know, Elihu chuckles inwardly. The kid has it in him to joke. He looks at Ethan's face to see where its joke-prone leanings reside.

Ethan either takes in the look and ignores it or doesn't pick up on it at all. He says, "She asked me if I wanted to be a writer."

"Annoying question, I know," Elihu says. "The kind of question adults always ask children. They figure all kids are likely to want to do what their parents do. She doesn't know our situation, of course."

"Yes, she asked me," Ethan says, "but you answered for me."

"I guess I did," Elihu says and regrets using the noncommittal "guess." Inwardly, something pokes him. "You *don't* want to be a writer, do you?"

"No," Ethan says, again with no special timbre. "No, I don't want to be a writer, but I could have answered for myself."

For the first time—the firsts are adding up—Elihu sees he has overstepped bounds and wonders whether the bounds over which he so proprietarily stepped are father-son bounds. He says, "Yes, you could have. It wasn't my place. I apologize."

Ethan neither accepts nor rejects the apology. He gives a minimal nod and resumes eating for a minute or two. Then he looks up from his plate and says, "That was pretty funny when that woman called me Ethan Goulding. Too funny for me to correct her. You must of thought it was funny, too, since you didn't say anything."

"I didn't say anything," Elihu inserts, "because it would have meant more explaining. I didn't want to talk to her any longer than absolutely necessary."

"The funny thing is," Ethan says, although he says it without any hint of a smile, "is that when Emily told me about you, I tried out the name. To myself. Ethan Goulding. It didn't sound right. I'm used to Ethan Haas. It's as good a name as any. I even thought if I was Ethan Goulding, people might ask me if I'm related to Elihu Goulding. What would I say to that?"

He looks at Elihu to see if he has an answer. Elihu doesn't, so he says, "I guess I could say I'm his son, but I don't even know if I have the right. It sounds stupid to say I'm his biological son." Ethan gets an odd look on his features and says, "I guess I could say I'm his bastard son, couldn't I?"

Elihu suspects this is said to rile him. He knows he must respond to it. "You could say that. It's true by definition. But I hope you wouldn't. We've only just met, but it hadn't yet occurred to me that I've now met my bastard son. Edmund in *King Lear* is a bastard son. It seems to me 'bastard' has taken on connotations that don't fit you. From the little I know of you. The way with which manners and mores have been tinkered with over the last fifty years the word 'bastard' hardly has any traction anymore. 'Bastard' hits the ear as antiquated. A gag line in a *Saturday Night Live* skit."

"I guess I know what you mean," Ethan replies. I don't think of myself as a bastard. I don't know what would happen if I began to."

"Don't begin to," Elihu says. He had the mild inclination to reach out and put his hand over Ethan's. He resists it. Why? Did he have to stop himself?

For the twenty or so more minutes the dinner goes on—including a tartufo for Ethan—they say little other than things like "Could I have the milk?" and "How's the coffee?" As if either of them cares how the coffee is.

Elihu pays the bill. Ethan thanks him for the meal. They walk with determined strides to 73 East Ninth Street. They walk almost as if they're trying to outstrip each other. When they close the forest-green door behind them, Ethan says he's ready to hit the hay. Elihu says he'll be going up to the top floor to do some reading before turning in.

Thus ends the first day that Ethan avails himself of Elihu's ambivalent hospitality.

xiii.

Elihu does not quite see that Ethan and he fall into a routine. He wouldn't say they give each other a wide berth. It's more as if they become two men with not a great deal in common living in the same boarding house. Elihu lends some thought to this and assumes that such intimate estrangement may be common to fathers and sons—not that he's feeling particularly paternal. He has no way of knowing what Ethan is feeling. He doesn't ask.

There seems to be no question that Ethan is in the house to stay. Proof could be that Elihu hands Ethan the keys he had made for Mrs. Woolard but never gave her. Elihu falls into the habit of making breakfast many days. For other days he asks Ethan if he's partial to any cereals and lays in a few cartons of Kellogg's products. He keeps milk on hand. He does the shopping, as anyone would do for a houseguest. Or a boarder. He doubles up on other staples in order for Ethan to help himself to lunch. Some days they show up in the kitchen at the same time. Other days, if either Elihu or Ethan are not at home around lunchtime, they don't.

They do fall into the habit of eating out for dinner. Never again at Gene's—at other restaurants where the dark corners are now even more reassuring to Elihu. As the weeks pass, they encounter no more Ginger ("Ginge") Hochmans, although Elihu has something he regards as a much closer call. One March evening on their way to a Second Avenue restaurant, they're waiting for the traffic light to turn green when Elihu looks at the other side of Third Avenue and sees someone he thinks could be Bartlett Norcross. He's talking to two other men. Elihu isn't certain this is Bart, but he doesn't want to take the chance it might be. They would have to cross paths. They would have to speak. Too awkward, too much to explain—or too much he would leave unexplained. No matter how briefly they spoke, it would be disturbingly, embarrassingly superficial. Just the sort of small talk Elihu despises. Of all people to run into. To almost run into. Putting his hand on his left cheek, rubbing it and therefore obscuring his face, he looks again at the man he is all but certain has to be Bart. A Bart who has put on weight, if indeed he *is* Bart. Elihu assures himself he hasn't been seen.

But what can he do to avoid an encounter now that the light is changing? He turns on his heel, saying to Ethan he's left his wallet at the house and needs to get it. Ethan is surprised but no more than passingly affected. Elihu's plan is that he'll get farther down the block and, glancing backward as casually as he can rally, will track Bart and companions. If they head in another direction or into a building, he'll tell Ethan he's just realized he put his wallet in a different pocket than usual. He'll pat the pocket to signal he has it. They'll proceed to the evening's restaurant.

Which is what happens, and all goes smoothly enough. The dinner conversation is spare. Elihu asks Ethan what he's done during the day. Ethan replies with sketchy descriptions. The exchanges are hardly more informative than "Where did you go? Out. What did you do? Nothing." Elihu doesn't press for fuller details.

One evening over steaks—Elihu has learned Ethan has a taste for a good steak; what growing boy doesn't?—Ethan says he was at Fifth Avenue and Forty-Second Street, saw the Public Library and went in. This intrigues Elihu, but he somehow intuits, rightly or wrongly, that Ethan doesn't want to say more on the subject. "I did some reading there" is all he supplies. What on earth is Ethan reading, Elihu asks himself. He doesn't ask Ethan.

When Ethan isn't out during the day, he spends much of the time in his room. Elihu realizes he has come to regard the second-floor front bedroom as "his," as Ethan's room. He tried not to. He lets it go. Ethan vacates the bedroom to sit in the kitchen when Mrs. Woolard is cleaning. (Ethan is introduced to Mrs. Woolard as Elihu's son, in town for a short visit.) Otherwise, he's usually in the bedroom with the door closed, doing what, Elihu has no idea. One day Elihu passes the bedroom when the door is ajar several inches. The slice of room he is able to see tells him little or nothing. He sees a boot lying on its side and what looks like part of a towel hanging on the inside doorknob. Nothing revelatory. He thinks to peek in but doesn't. He thinks about knocking on the door but doesn't. He continues upstairs to read.

There is the bathroom situation. Two men sharing the same bathroom is not ideal. For one thing, Elihu realizes he has to keep a closer eye on the toilet paper rolls. He's taken to leaving a couple of extras handy. Ethan leaves his dopp kit in the bathroom. Although his beard is thick, as Elihu's is, he doesn't shave every day. He gets whisker-y, which Elihu recognizes as standard for young men these days. He flashes on Ethan and him shaving side by side as younger father and younger son. Elihu wonders if Ethan has the same irritating problem shaving his cleft chin. He never asks. When they were younger and together, would he have shown Ethan his technique?

It isn't that Ethan and he say nothing at all to each other. Besides the amenities, he receives the occasional travel report on Ethan's exploits in the city. Not only to the Forty-Second Street library. Ethan says, "I went to the Statue of Liberty this morning" or "I went to Ellis Island this afternoon. It was the way you wrote about it in *The Accidental Immigrants.*" (Yes, Ethan *had* read all three Elihu Goulding novels, even closely. Had that piece of information slipped out, or was it deliberately stated?) "I went to Radio City Music Hall," Ethan said one late afternoon. "What a tourist trap. I guess I shouldn't be surprised." Ethan liked the Metropolitan Museum. That's to say he "got something" from the art, but again was more entertained "by how the tourists behaved. They walked right past great paintings by artists they didn't know to get to paintings by artists they did know. To them the only artist really worth knowing is Van Gogh. And all they really know about him is he chopped off his ear."

Because Ethan is getting himself around, Elihu wonders how he's paying for it. He didn't seem to have had much money when he was on the road to 73 East Ninth Street. Elihu offers Ethan money two or three times. It's what a father does, isn't it? So there are times when Elihu takes that approach.

Ethan turns the offers down the first few times they're made, but after several turn-downs, he accepts fifty dollars. Elihu has the impression that Ethan takes the cash more from giving Elihu satisfaction than from any need. Subsequently, he accepts more offers. Somewhere in there, Elihu has a brief thought that he's handing Ethan the weekly allowance he would have been giving him had he been involved with the boy's upbringing. He puts that thought aside, preferring to take the attitude that if Ethan is not sitting in the house, not sitting in the bedroom in the house, he needs to be encouraged to do more along those lines.

For there are days when Ethan doesn't leave the house, days when Elihu sees him only at breakfast, if even then, and at dinner when they go somewhere close by. He assumes Ethan is in the front bedroom behind the closed door and has not slipped out. He hears nothing, no music, no footfalls. Perhaps once or twice a day, he passes by the bathroom and the door is closed, which it is only when one of them is using it—which has become their sign to each other. When Elihu was alone in the house, he never thought to close the door. When Mrs. Woolard was there, he avoided using the bathroom until she had left. Now he goes by and might hear water splashing in the basin or the shower going or the toilet flushing.

Since it's now April and the New York spring weather has become mild, even milder than forecasts report it normally is, he sometimes leaves the kitchen door leading to the garden open, with only a screen door he has had repaired closed. A few times he checks outside to see if Ethan might be spending a few minutes or even an hour there, possibly seated on the metal bench at the bottom of the newly leafy space. Elihu had found a local gardener, a youngster, really, who calls himself Dooley (first name or surname, Elihu didn't bother to ascertain). Dooley cleans the garden and even establishes beds along the fences on both sides. At Elihu's request and because he is not interested in upkeep, Dooley has planted perennials.

Ethan is never in the garden, nor does he take advantage of other rooms in the house. Elihu invites Ethan to visit the third floor if he has any desire to read and wants to avail himself of the books there. He does this reluctantly. He will feel crowded at setting another precedent. It's a safe offer. As far as he knows, Ethan, who did say he wasn't much of a reader, doesn't seize the opportunity. Evidently, the only reading he's done was during his Public Library stop. As far as Elihu knows, Ethan has never brought a book into the house—or pulled one from his backpack.

To be exact, Ethan hasn't seized the opportunity to take any books, but Elihu is aware of Ethan coming upstairs at least once after that first day. This happens in the middle of the night. When this occurs, Elihu is not certain what time it is. Since there's no clock in the library-study and he hardly ever wears his watch in the house, time remaining a useless commodity—and the library-study (the entire house really) having become his version of timelessness—the correct or approximate time is at best a guess.

He does know that Ethan's unique third-floor appearance is well into the wee hours. As Elihu so often does, he has fallen asleep in the club chair. He has not turned off the reading lamp, hasn't closed the book. He's reading Stendhal's *The Red and the Black* in a translation he considers dubious. The volume is askew on his lap, the page he was reading now creased. (Elihu does not like creased pages or broken spines, an oddball foible at a time when books in print are threatening to become passé. Are already passé?)

Elihu must be sleeping lightly, because he is awakened from a dream he immediately forgets. Jolted up and leaning around the chair to look down the room, he sees Ethan. Ethan in his white T-shirt and white boxer shorts and bare-footed, standing in the shadows like a deer caught on the road.

"Oh," Ethan says, "I didn't know you were still up here. I thought you forgot to turn the light off. I'll leave you alone." He starts to turn away.

Elihu stops him. "Stay. You can stay. Did you come up to get a book?"

Ethan remains where he is. "No, it's just I couldn't sleep."

"Then take a book," Elihu suggests. "Books can put you to sleep. It happens to me all the time." He considers making a crack about the effect his own books have of putting him to sleep. It would be a lie. He doesn't read them, so they can't put him to sleep. He holds up *The Red and the Black*. "Henri-Marie Beyle, better known as Stendhal, just had me snoozing. Or his translator did."

When he says that, he asks himself why he had to throw in the piece of literary pedantry. Henri-Marie Beyle! He could have simply said "Stendhal just did it for me." He suspects anyone else would have kept things succinct. Does he think he's going to add to Ethan's education, perhaps fill in some lapses Ethan has suffered as a Yale dropout? Does he suddenly think it's a father's place? Is he suddenly, without thinking about it, assuming paternal duties? Baloney.

Again starting to turn, Ethan says, "I should go back to bed and let you get back to Stendhal." Elihu notices that Ethan leaves out the Henri-Marie Beyle part. "I had to read it for a course once. It was okay."

Only okay, Elihu thinks. That could almost pass for an opinion, Ethan's having placed *The Red and the Black* somewhere slightly below the level of his *Wandering Youth*, et cetera, assessments. But if Ethan read the Stendhal classic, did that indicate he was taking literature classes? Had he been majoring in literature? Elihu didn't want to ask.

He wouldn't have had time, anyway. Ethan is turning back and, surprisingly, moves a step or two out of the shadows and closer to the circle of light spilling from the lamp. He says, "It's just I couldn't get to sleep. I thought I'd come up here and look out at the garden. You know, the moon, the stars."

Elihu says, "This is New York City. We don't have any stars."

Ethan does something Elihu hasn't yet seen him do. He laughs. It's not a sustained laugh. It comes and goes quickly, rather like the joke Ethan offered some days before. But it's a laugh with a guttural masculine lilt. Not only that. In its brevity, Ethan hears something familiar. It takes a few seconds for him to place it. It is an echo of Emily Haas's laugh. No wonder he doesn't recognize it instantly. He hasn't heard its like in over twenty years.

It prompts him to ask Ethan, "Why can't you sleep?"

Ethan begins to take another step closer but steps back. "I don't know. You know. It happens." Standing where he is, he says, "I can probably fall asleep now." He points behind him. "I should probably get going." He says it, but he doesn't move.

Elihu notices and says, "You must have some idea why you can't sleep. When I can't sleep, I can probably come up with four or five reasons why." Over the years, Elihu has long lost count of his sleepless nights.

"Sometimes it's a combination of all of them. What do you think is on your mind?"

Again Ethan resumes the look of a docile animal held at bay. He says nothing for several seconds. When they've passed as if they were attenuated minutes, he says, "I'd better get back to bed. I'm sure I can fall asleep now."

He turns and goes, his broad-shouldered, thick-necked, thick-thighed body swallowed up in the dark at the other end of the room.

Elihu is conflicted about stopping him. Should he? Should he not? Should he go after Ethan? What is the right thing to do when there are no shoulds? What is the paternal thing to do? He doesn't know. He says nothing, just turns back, gazes out the window, where there are no stars, and finds the passage in *The Red and the Black* where he dozed off. He reads and does not doze off again so precipitately.

xiv.

A few days later, having thought more about Ethan's housebound tendency, having thought more about Ethan's sleeping difficulty (if only the one time, as far as he knows), Elihu gets an idea. He'll suggest another venture for the two of them. He considers referring to it as an adventure but regards that as too cute. He holds off. He'll suggest the outing but let Ethan decide what course it should take.

Raising the prospect, he asks what Ethan has not seen in New York City that he still wants to see. Ethan answers but in such a way that Elihu gets the feeling he's the one being humored. "How about a ball game?" pops out of Elihu's mouth. Where did that come from? Elihu knows: from the clutch of outings fathers are supposed to take with sons. For a second, Elihu is surprised he hadn't suggested going fishing. Not that he ever did with Morris or ever thought about doing himself. Since it's April, he wouldn't have brought up skiing.

Ethan shakes his head with some show of thought and says, "I'm not that into baseball. I've wanted to see the 9/11 Memorial." He stops, then talks on with a lingering look of uncertainty on his fleshy, stubbly face, "But I don't know."

It's something to go on, Elihu thinks. Okay, if the 9/11 Memorial is what Ethan wants even hesitantly, Elihu—who has gone on no jaunts to update himself on New York City since he last lived here—decides fine, sure, let's do that. It so happens that visiting the revised site of the Twin Towers catastrophe is just the sort of tourist-y outing he has always disdained. More than that, he has his private response to the invasion that has to do with cosmeticized memorials of any stripe. He thinks back on his horror at once taking the train from Munich to Dachau and observing what had been done there to turn a death camp into a green field with a bland, wooden "Arbeit Macht Frei" sign over the entrance and tidy buildings here and there.

But he'll go to the memorial. Sometimes, he tells himself, a parent does what his child favors, even an adult child. He'll go in that frame of mind, in a parent's frame of mind.

On the next warm spring Thursday, when the trees are showing celadon buds and tulips and daffodils are boldly raising their heads, Elihu and Ethan walk the mile or so down Fifth Avenue, through Washington Square Park, through the Village, Soho, Tribeca, over to Church Street. The walk is decided on this way:

Elihu: "Do you want to take the subway? Or we could walk."

Ethan with little affect: "We can walk."

They are men of few words. In what has become predictable, the words exchanged between them remain few. The two of them have become the essence of terse. Elihu says, "Nice spring day, isn't it?" and wonders if he's blushing at the bromide. It's years ago he made a hard-and-fast practice of avoiding bromides. He's also wary of "hard-and-fast."

Ethan manages, "Yeah, it is…a nice day," and after a pause, "I don't know why I thought this, but I didn't expect spring in New York to be like everywhere else."

"What did you think it would be like?"

"I don't know. Grimy. No flowers anywhere." He leaves it at that.

They leave it at that. Elihu gives a minute or two over to imagining of what a grimy, flower-free Manhattan spring would consist. Nothing comes to him. He thinks, "That probably attests to my mind for fiction having irrevocably dried up."

Elihu and Ethan are monosyllabic at the memorial as well, but the mood has a different heft. Elihu does not know how to gauge it as Ethan and he walk around the pools where silence or, at most, modulated voices are the order of the solemn environment. People speak quietly to one another and stop to pose for pictures.

Elihu understands the behavior and yet picks up something different from Ethan. Ethan stops once in a while as they walk. He sits on the low walls or bends down by them. He reads the etched names of the hijacked airplanes' victims. He reads them to himself. Elihu watches Ethan's mouth—the mouth shaped so like his own—shaping the names. Sometimes Ethan pronounces part of a name so softly as to be all but inaudible. Elihu hears "…bert" for, he assumes, "Robert" or "Marion A.…" With each partially pronounced name Ethan clenches his mouth and almost imperceptibly shakes his head. His dark eyes (Elihu's eyes) grow misty. He retreats into himself.

Elihu cannot read Ethan's reactions. At the same time, he doesn't feel he should interrupt Ethan to ask what he thinks of the memorial. He has the distinct impression that Ethan is responding to the surroundings more profoundly (is "profoundly" the right word?), more emotionally (if "emotionally" is another applicable word) than Elihu might have expected. Much of what Ethan has reported about other landmarks he has visited has left few lasting impressions on Elihu. He wonders if this one will.

Following Ethan's path, Elihu completes a slow, forty-five-minute walk around the pools and along the paths with their only recently planted young trees. He knows it's been forty-five minutes because he checked his watch. Throughout that duration, Ethan has barely looked back at Elihu, who has deliberately remained three or four feet behind him.

(Elihu and watches: This isn't the first time he's slid one on his right wrist since he's been back in Manhattan. The watch he owns—he inherited—is his father's Elgin, a relic with an expanding gold band. As he has often remarked to himself, "My time is my own, so no need to wear a watch." Since Ethan arrived, however, he's taken to wearing the watch occasionally to remind himself when he wants his solitude back. Or what now passes for solitude.)

After the approximate forty-five minutes, Ethan stops, turns to peer at Elihu, holds whatever thought he has and after several seconds says, "Wow." Only that. "Wow."

Elihu is almost, but not quite, inured to the incessant "wow!" use of people young and old. He always thinks of the vocal palindrome as a disturbing example of woefully limited expression. (Likewise, he regards the unstoppable fallback on obscenities. He refuses to be caught saying "fuck" or "fucking," except when referring to the actual act, and then sparingly. After all, he has so few occasions to do so. He disliked hearing it from Ethan the one time he did hear it but held his disapproving tongue.)

"Wow!" with its strongly implied exclamation point is another example of his preferring to read alone indoors rather than face the world. "Wow!" doesn't very often crop up in the literature to which he pays attention. That's to say, it never does.

But, Elihu muses now, the ubiquitous "wow!" is usually spoken with an edge of excitement, of appreciation, of a desire to share whatever the "wow!" inducing experience is.

The "wow" that Ethan has just emitted is not that. It's uttered with no trace of an accompanying exclamation point. Elihu finds anything but excitement in Ethan's invoking the threadbare outburst. There is astonishment in Ethan's use but astonishment infused with melancholy, with sadness, even with despair, defeat. It's as if an invisible veil has fallen over Ethan's face. Intent on learning more about Ethan's take, Elihu says, "I suppose 'wow!' is the only response." He pointedly attaches the exclamation point.

He hears the sarcasm in his comment, but Ethan doesn't seem to, or, if he does, disregards it. Instead, he lowers his head, which shifts his springy hair in the slight spring breeze. He raises his head slowly again so that he's looking at the sky. He swivels his head about seventy degrees and says, "Those buildings were here, and now they're gone. All those people. Lost. Gone. Jumping from smashed windows. If something like what happened here can happen, what's it all for, anyway?" He lowers his head and points around him with his left-hand index finger. "What good is all this? It doesn't bring anything back. Does it?" He puts the "does it?" in spoken boldface. "It's like a sop to the living. We're supposed to honor memories here, but what we're really remembering is something horrible, unthinkable. It makes you wonder. Not in any kind of good way."

Besides being surprised—surprised by the restrained passion Ethan is expressing—Elihu takes this in as the longest statement Ethan has made since he arrived.

He doesn't know how to answer it but senses he ought to. Has to. But because he has similar, if not exactly the same, responses to the memorial, he hasn't an immediate response. "I know what you mean," he says following several seconds in which they're both silent, "but I don't think the place is as…bleak as you seem to."

("Bleak" is a word that years before Elihu decided was one of the most beautiful in the English language. For that reason he's chosen to use it rarely. He did seed it into both *Wandering Youth* and *For My Betters*, once in each. His using it just then seemed exactly appropriate.)

"Oh, no?" Ethan says. "Not as bleak? Do you think this is all sweetness and light?" He waved his heavy arm to take in the scope of the surroundings.

"I didn't say that," Elihu says, "but I do believe the people who put the memorial together had their hearts in the right place." Elihu hears himself fall back on yet another bromide.

"So what?" Ethan replies. He waits for Elihu to answer him. When Elihu offers no response, he says, "What does that mean anyway? 'Their hearts in the right place.' A lot of evil is pulled off by people who have their hearts in the right place. My guess is they never got that their hearts were really in the wrong place. The way wrong place." Ethan stands up, in a state Elihu takes to be defiant, yet abashed. His broad shoulders are hunched. He says, "I'm ready to get out of here."

Which they do, skipping the adjacent museum. At first saying little, they walk back to East Ninth Street. As they advance with a matching slow but steady, all but funereal pace, Elihu decides the thing to do is leave Ethan to his thoughts, however despondent they might be. He says nothing until about halfway towards home Ethan suddenly turns to him and cries out—right there in the street—"You can go to that place and just take it in? That's it? That's all you, you know? That's all you feel?"

Noticing one or two pedestrians they're passing stop to look at Ethan, Elihu responds faintly, "Perhaps I feel it differently from you. You understand that."

"I don't," Ethan replies.

Shaking his head as if in solemn objection, he again falls silent.

Elihu is tempted to try cheering the boy up but decides it's some years since his cheering-up wherewithal has been shipshape. If it's gloom Ethan wants to nurture, let him have it. After all, Ethan is young. Sooner or later, he's bound to cheer himself up.

XV.

That's where Elihu is wrong—radically wrong, as it turns out. If he had retained the deft fiction writer's eye, ear and insight, he would have known as much. He has already registered Ethan's pensiveness, his constant introspection, the solemnity in the boy that only seemed exacerbated by the 9/11 Memorial trip. He hasn't registered—he'd previously had no opportunity to—Ethan's deeper discontent.

He is handed the opportunity.

The night after Ethan and he return from the memorial, Elihu has fallen asleep in the back bedroom on the second floor, a rare occasion since Ethan started bunking in. Elihu is awakened by the sound of singing—Ethan, apparently now in his bedroom.

Elihu looks at the clock on the left end table, where he'd also placed Turgenev's *Fathers and Sons*, a book he'd chosen to reread, he suspects, less for uncomplicated pleasure than for its possible hints on parenting. (Shortly after the incident when he'd seen Bart Norcross in the street, he removed the photograph of Bart and him on the right end table. If for any reason Ethan were to see it, there might be more explanations required. No need for that.)

It's 2:18, and Ethan is in his bedroom singing what Elihu makes out as a frighteningly off-pitch version of the Rolling Stones' "You Can't Always Get What You Want." Just the chorus, raggedly repeated enough to get Elihu out of bed in his underwear. He thinks to put on a bathrobe. It's not by the hook on the bedroom door. He isn't certain where he hung it last. Is it upstairs on the club chair? The hell with it.

He leaves the room and goes to Ethan's, where the door is open and Ethan, sitting on the bed while trying to remove his pants, is exhaling "But if you try sometimes, you just might get what you need." Then again, "But if you try sometimes, you just might get what you need." Then again, "But if you try some—."

Seeing Elihu in the door, Ethan cuts himself off and says, "Hey, Dad, do you think it's true, that if you try sometimes, you just might get what you need?"

Elihu doesn't like this at all. "You're drunk," he says.

"Well, get that," Ethan says, one chunky leg out of his pants, the other still in. "The novelist's powers of observation on full display. Yeah, I'm drunk. I'm tanked. I'm pissed. I'm three sheets to the wind. I'm shit-faced. And I don't even drink. What are you going to do about it? Gimme a lecture? You can't, Dad, and you know why? 'Cause you're not my dad. When have you ever been a dad to me? Never. Not by choice. I had to show up here, practically begging for hospitality."

Anger rising rapidly in Elihu's craw and possibly to the breaking point, he says, "I'll lecture you—if you think this is a lecture—because this is my house, and you're in it. You're a guest in it. You're not welcome to come home—I mean, here—drunk at two o'clock in the morning."

"Is it only two? Wow! I thought it was later." Elihu notices the spark in the "wow" that he hadn't heard when Ethen invoked it that afternoon. No, yesterday afternoon. "I could've stayed out later and come home—I mean here—even drunker." Elihu doesn't miss the sarcasm in the "I mean, here." He knows he isn't meant to.

"Maybe I'll go back to whatever bar I was in last. Maybe not. I think I was thrown out of that one. Maybe I'll go back to the one before that. If I can remember where it is. Who gives a shit? I'll find a new one."

The thought crossing Elihu's mind is, he's not about to tolerate this.

"For all I care, you can go and not come back," he says. Listening to himself say that, he's immediately uncertain. Boys get drunk. He knows that. He never did, but Seth Levy did. In *Wandering Youth* he created a drunk episode as a dramatic effect deviating from the novel's more strictly autobiographical thrust. He was fictionalizing. There were likewise other deviations to throw readers off his scent. The same for Sabe Levensohn in *For My Betters*—the intermittent deviation giving him the cover to deny he was writing about himself. ("Of course, Seth Levy isn't me," he'd say and laugh a bemused laugh. "Of course, Sabe Levensohn isn't me," he'd say. "I've never been much of a drinker, but I've had many friends who were.")

Ethan is giving the abrupt eviction notice a few seconds' thought. "Maybe that's what I'll do," he blurts. "I'll get out of here. Yeah, that's it. I'll get out of here. Why shouldn't I? I'm not getting anything out of being here. I thought I'd come and find my dad, my real father. I ain't found anything like that. You're not my dad in anything other than a single—what do they call 'em—in anything more than a single protozoa." He has trouble getting the word out and laughs at himself for it. "Big deal. I mean, small deal. Really small deal." He puts his left thumb and forefinger together, leaving an infinitesimal space. "Much, much smaller than that," he says. His thick fingers are slightly trembling. "That's what I'll do. Get the fuck out of here. The fucking Rolling Stones, fucking Mick Jagger doesn't know what he's talking about. If you try sometimes, you still don't get what you need."

"Then get out," Elihu says, without trying to stop himself. "Pack your things, and get out. I'll give you enough money for a cab to Penn Station or Grand Central. Your choice."

"With pleasure," Ethan garbles and stands up. Or tries to. As his pants are half on and half off, he puts one socked foot on them, attempts to take a step, loses his already precarious balance and falls on the bed.

"I'll get up and go in a few minutes," he mumbles, and then, just as he falls asleep on the unmade bed, he says, "You're not my fucking dad. You're not my fucking dad. You'll never be my—." His eyes close slowly. He's sleeping. He begins to snore. Violently.

Elihu pulls a blanket from under Ethan and covers him. This wakes Ethan enough for him to utter, "You'll never be—."

In the morning, neither the memorial trip nor its next-night aftermath is mentioned again by Ethan or Elihu. Does Ethan have the slightest recollection of it? That's unclear. Elihu somehow knows not bringing it up is the right way to handle it. Let sleeping dogs lie is the appropriate bromide for the unfortunate occasion.

Moreover, Elihu thinks—knows—he's complicit in the heat of the inebriant wee-hours exchange. Quite aware that Ethan was in no shape to go anywhere, why did he say what he said? What did he think he would accomplish by threatening, by issuing an eviction notice he certainly didn't mean? Did he? What, he wants to know, is at the bottom of his sudden anger? Where did it come from? It seems to have erupted from a previously untapped segment of his core. He can't remember the last time he gave in to such rage. He's not convinced there is a precedent.

As to Ethan's tastes in music, Elihu thinks he's apparently heard the Rolling Stones at least once.

xvi.

Things remain the same for the next few days, perhaps for a week or more. Ethan's behavior seems the same—or perhaps a minimal degree or two worse. Aside from assiduously clocking Ethan's routine, Elihu estimates Ethan is spending less time outside the house and more time in the house, in the front bedroom.

 Contemplating his surmise around three weeks on, Elihu gives some thought to whether or not he ought to ask Ethan something, try to get the boy to talk more about himself. Come to think of it, Elihu gauged, Ethan had said little. Could be enough time had passed for asking Ethan to express more about how he felt at the memorial. It's clear, Elihu thinks, that Ethan was feeling something more than he revealed. Or maybe it would be safer, less provocative—gentler—to ask Ethan what his plans, if any, might be.

 Elihu hopes Ethan has plans, despite his not yet mentioning any. But the repeated threat does linger in the air. He's aware of it, if Ethan isn't. If Ethan is considering leaving, Elihu thinks about giving the boy money for his travels, for maybe a journey to "find himself," which Elihu is well aware has been a customary pastime for young men and women generation after generation. Hadn't he made hay of the familiar "he's-finding-himself" trek? There it is in the title of *Wandering Youth*, not that nowadays he puts much stock in his—as he chooses to regard the volumes—juvenilia.

 He hasn't made the hard-cash offer yet, because he realizes it can come across as a double-edged gift. The more cutting edge could be the implication that money is a bribe to get rid of Ethan. That's an insult Elihu is not prepared to inflict again. Anything but that.

As a few weeks pass and May is ending, Elihu begins keeping a closer watch on Ethan. He notices that Ethan has recently been going out only to return within a half hour or so, saying nothing but the barest amenities and often carrying a small paper bag the contents of which are a mystery to Elihu. Ethan is the same at meals. On the couple of occasions Elihu has suggested going somewhere for lunch or dinner, if for no other reason than setting up a situation where more conversation might develop, Ethan has responded he would just as soon stay in. He's polite, but he demurs. He leaves his room only on the day Mrs. Woolard comes in. When Mrs. Woolard is gone, Elihu assumes, Ethan speedily returns to the tidied zone he prefers.

One early June afternoon when the temperature has shot up, Elihu thinks he might use the humidity-laden change to ask Ethan if the air conditioner in the front bedroom is operating properly. Elihu traditionally disdains air conditioners. He thinks that, installed in wall sleeves, they're, at best, unaesthetic. When he lives in the country, he always rents houses with no air conditioning, an easy enough requirement to meet. When he lives in the city, he tolerates air conditioners so long as he doesn't have to turn them on. He likes open windows. If he sweats, he sweats. Perspiration is human, he insists to himself and, on the odd occasion, to others. When he was still writing, he liked it when he would sweat in front of the typewriter. He liked that he was literally sweating the novels out. On East Ninth Street, he finds the cross-draft created by open windows in the front and back of the house as, if not entirely refreshing, at least livable.

Livable for him. Ethan may not have the same proclivity. Maybe Ethan likes air conditioning but could be having trouble with the blasted machine in his room. It could be. Elihu wouldn't know. He has never tried any of the ones in the house. Why would he? He hadn't thought about contacting servicemen to prepare them for summer. That's a spring-cleaning routine for which he has never had any regard. If you don't like air conditioners, you get to scoff at the people who claim they can't live without them. He's done his share of scoffing.

The air conditioner explanation is, if Elihu is candid with himself, merely an excuse to go into what he has come more and more to think of as Ethan's bedroom. He cannot put his finger on it precisely, but he has an inkling (funny word for what's more like a gnawing concern) that something in the bedroom may not be entirely right. Not "kosher" is the Yiddish equivalent, Yiddishisms still popping up in him as a result of the unimpeachable Jean-Morris influence. He used to think humanity's curse of becoming one's parents was a canard. He's beginning to have his doubts. Still he's certain Ethan won't succumb, not in any manner, to becoming Elihu. How could he? He doesn't know who Elihu is.

So on this admittedly sweltering afternoon when only the most elusive breezes are moving through the house, Elihu decides he'll talk to the boy. That's what the good parent does, isn't it? He can assume that role tentatively, he says to himself as he heads to Ethan's door from the library-study where he's been mulling this.

The door, as he noticed earlier, is closed. Not an unusual condition. He knocks on it lightly. No response. He knocks more heavily. Still no response. He leans towards the door frame and says, "Ethan, it's Elihu." He hears nothing. He says, "Ethan, it's Eli"—he hasn't referred to himself as Eli since he can't remember when. "May I come in? I'd like to come in."

Silence. Elihu is losing patience with the unresponsive kid. He thinks to say, "Ethan, it's your father. I would like you to open the door." He doesn't say it. Saying so would admit to his parental responsibility. Saying so is what a father says to a son. He sees no call for that. He says only, and with calculated anger, "Ethan, open the door, or I'll have to open it." That's what a homeowner, or in his case, a renter, says.

When this still induces no response, he reaches for the doorknob, turns it and pushes. It does not open. There is little give. Something is blocking the door, he realizes with a start. He pushes harder. Whatever the something is begins to give. The door opens wider until Elihu is able to angle himself sideways into the room. He sees that a heavy chair he has had with him over many relocations is the obstacle.

He also sees that the curtains on both windows facing the street have been pulled tight so that no strong southern light can enter the room. This has only compounded the June heat. The blocked light forcing its way through the thin curtains gives the room a deep purple glimmer.

It is light enough that Elihu sees Ethan on the bed. He's lying on his side in the position Elihu has seen before. He is wearing the usual white T-shirt, bunched up to reveal his hairy belly, the boxer shorts. His legs are splayed. His left arm is lying across his chest. His right arm is above him on the pillow as if reaching for something just beyond his grasp. He appears to be deeply asleep.

"Ethan," Elihu calls. When that has no effect, he calls in capital letters, "Ethan, Ethan, wake up, I want to talk to you." Which also prompts nothing, no movement whatsoever.

Now angrier, Elihu takes a few determined steps to the bed. As he approaches, he spots something—some things—on the table at the right side of the bed. Small bottles. There are many of them. Ten? A dozen? Elihu doesn't stop to count them but—more than curious—picks one up. It's a plastic bottle containing ten-milligram Melatonin, a Nature's Sun product. He shakes it. It's empty. Elihu has heard about Melatonin but has no idea what it's for. He has had the impression that it's something homeopathic taken by health nuts towards whom he's only ever had a bemused, dismissive attitude. He reads the label, where the word "sleep-inducing" not only catches his eye but virtually stings it. With all due speed, he puts down that bottle and picks up one after another, all of them boasting ten-milligram Melatonin, some Nature's Sun, others other brands, each one empty. He picks up one that is not Melatonin but is a benzodiazepine alternative that claims to have effective sleep-inducing characteristics.

Noticing another bottle that's fallen to the floor, Elihu feels anger infused with fear flush through his frame. He's dimly aware of a third emotion, which he thinks for an evaporating instant could be concern. Aloud, he says to the possibly unconscious Ethan, "No, you don't. Not on *my* time."

He's lost as to what to do. What do you do when something like this happens? You call 911. He considers going to the phone. Damn, he's seen to it that the only phone in the house is in the kitchen. (He's never changed his attitude towards owning a cell phone.) To race downstairs he'd have to leave Ethan. He's reluctant to waste the time. And then what if there's a stretch before medical emergency help arrives? It may be too much of a chance.

He bends over to adjust the deeply sleeping Ethan so that he's on his back. Ethan is heavy. It takes effort to reposition him in order to grab his substantial shoulders and pull him up to a sitting position. Or attempt to. Ethan is dead weight. When that phrase hits Elihu, his mounting fear that Ethan could be dead builds. He puts considerable heft into raising Ethan. As he does, he starts pounding Ethan's back.

"Wake up," he demands. "Wake up," he pleads.

It comes to him that Ethan is still breathing. Ethan stirs for a few seconds. Elihu stops pounding Ethan's back. Now he slaps Ethan's face. He doesn't know if he's slapping for medical reasons or out of vengeful impulses. Ethan stirs again. He opens his eyes. His eyelids flutter.

His jaw drops. He emits a groggy, unintelligible sound. It sounds like "Wha…"

Elihu has Ethan by the shoulders again. He shakes him. He says, "You hear me, don't you, Ethan?" Ethan issues a variation on the "wha." Elihu says, "What do you think you're up to?" He does not expect an answer.

Nevertheless, he gets one, a slowly phrased, "I jus' wanna sleep. Lemme sleep." Saying that, Ethan tries to wrestle loose from Elihu. He's not able to. He hasn't the strength Elihu has.

"No sleeping, Ethan," Elihu says. "Waking up is what you're going to do." With that, he musters the additional strength to get himself up from the bed and pull Ethan up with him. When he does, he flings Ethan's right arm over his right shoulder and starts walking the drugged boy around the floor, skirting as best he can the various things Ethan has carelessly let drop there, kicking some of them out of the way.

Ethan tries to resist but can't. With Elihu holding him up like a five-foot-ten rag doll, he begins only slightly more steadily putting one foot in front of the other. After several minutes, Ethan, still giddy, begins to walk on his own. He's unsteady, but he's walking.

As he does, Elihu guides him to the chair by the door and sits him there. It is not his purpose to let Ethan return to the bed. Placing Ethan where he wants him—Ethan's arms on the arms of the chair, his head lolling—Elihu decides to act on a plan he's been formulating for the several minutes he's been walking the dazed boy.

Someone who has always given Elihu a good laugh—there haven't been many, not merely enough he's often contended—is W. C. Fields. Elihu has always been drawn to the Hollywood clowns of the twenties and thirties. He well knows the decades weren't a more innocent time, as they have so often been declared to be in succeeding decades, but he believes the screen comics were genuinely more innocent.

There's a 1934 Fields film that Elihu considers his favorite: *It's a Gift*. In it there's a sequence where Fields, living in a third-floor walk-up, goes out to the porch hoping to sleep. His hopes are dashed by interruptions that include a mother on the floor above the pajama-clad Fields and a daughter on the street bantering about whether the mother wants the daughter to shop for Ipecac or Syrup of Squills.

When Elihu—well, the adolescent Eli—first saw the movie, he had never heard of Ipecac or Syrup of Squills. He assumed they were silly-sounding names made up by Fields. He learned otherwise when years later he was in a Manhattan apothecary. Wandering about a store the likes of which was no longer commonplace, he suddenly saw something he never imagined he would see—a short shelf holding bottles of Ipecac. They appeared to be there more for display than for commercial purposes.

He grabbed one hastily. He had to have it—not for use, but for laughs. (He saw no Syrup of Squills bottles nearby.) He read that the contents were vomit inducing, but when would he ever need Ipecac for that purpose? He just liked knowing the bottle was in his medicine cabinet wherever he lived. A joke only he got. (Or maybe the rare guest peeking through the medicine cabinet, as some snooping guests have a habit of doing.) Every once in a while, he'd spot the Ipecac and rerun the Fields sequence in his head.

Right now Ipecac is no joke. After all these years, he has a use for it. That's if it is even effective, if it hasn't long ago passed its sell-by date. He'd had to do some fast talking to get the pharmacist to let him purchase it. "It's for display only," the man had said. "You have it," Elihu had said, "I ought to be able to buy it."

Leaving Ethan more or less upright in the chair, Elihu runs to the bathroom, relieved it's so convenient, retrieves the ancient bottle, astonished that that's what he's actually doing. Before leaving the bathroom, he takes the glass on the sink and fills it with water. He assumes that the aged mystery solution should not be consumed unadulterated. He opens the bottle, not an easy task, and pours what he figures is a spoonful of the potion into the glass.

He returns to Ethan, who hasn't shifted positions, raises the boy's heavy head and says, hearing himself dictate, as if in a bad movie, "Here. Drink this."

Ethan reflexively resists, but his reflexes aren't enough. He opens his mouth and swallows a few drops, coughs. His eyes blink, as if what he's swallowed is—is what? Bitter? Acidic? Elihu keeps administering the cloudy liquid. After a minute or two, Ethan has downed about half of the glass's contents and is more steadfastly resisting the rest.

Elihu relents. "Okay," he says. "Let's hope that's enough." Uncertain whether the Ipecac will have any effect and, if it does, how long it will take, he puts the glass on the floor and fetches the wastebasket from across the room. He is so determined that Ethan empty his stomach that he even considers putting a finger down Ethan's throat. Or somehow encouraging Ethan to put his own fingers down his throat. He decides against either alternative.

As yet, Ethan continues to be confused. With some effort, he shakes his head. His eyes blink, squint. He moans, weakly. This goes on for several minutes, with Elihu watching him closely should he pitch forward or harm himself physically in some manner.

During these sluggish minutes, Elihu is not thinking exclusively of Ethan but also of himself. How did he come to be in this situation? How does he feel about it? If this is what being a parent consists of, is it anything he's ever wanted? Is this boy anyone he ever wanted? Do Elihu's driven, concerted actions represent any other response than that of an apprehensive passerby, than that of a nodding acquaintance caught in a crisis where what he's done is the only thing he could have done, than that of someone who never expected to rely on W. C. Fields in this damnable far-fetched way?

Yes, his responses do represent something more dedicated, Elihu is admitting to himself, when, abruptly, Ethan pitches forward and begins regurgitating. Elihu doesn't immediately have the wastebasket strategically placed but wangles it there for most of Ethan's disturbing stomach contents. Included in the mephitic contents are the hints of recent meals Elihu has no interest in identifying. He'd like to turn away, hold his nose or his breath, but it's more urgent that he hold Ethan's head to keep it from veering off target.

The upheavals abate and resume a half-dozen times. Elihu repositions himself in front of Ethan. He watches his boy's face bulge, retract, change shape. For Elihu, it's as if he's watching his own face transformed into a Francis Bacon portrait. Curiouser and curiouser, he thinks.

Finally, when both Elihu and Ethan are satisfied that all is purged, Elihu, aware he is tired of standing all this time, sits on the arm of the chair.

Ethan looks to be coming to more of his senses. As he does, he looks at Elihu and says, "I'm sorry. I'm sorry. I'm sorry." There are tears in his eyes.

Elihu cannot tell if they're tears implying emotion or just part of the physical stress.

"I'm sorry," Ethan repeats.

"It's all right," Elihu says. Not knowing what else to do to comfort the boy, he puts his arms around him. In return, Ethan puts his arms around Elihu. Both of them—realizing what they've done, embarrassed by what they've impulsively done—pull back.

Again Ethan says, "I'm sorry," but it's uncertain whether he's regretting the unprecedented hug or the flustered activity that preceded it.

Equally unsure of what has just transpired, Elihu says, "Don't worry about it." He thinks he's referring to the suicide attempt—and that's the first time he's allowed himself to consider the term. The foolish suicide attempt, he amends it in his mind. Or is he referring to the spontaneous hug rather than the massive pill intake? Both still have him provoked.

Then Ethan says something Elihu is not ready for. Not that he's prepared for any of this. Who comes prepared for anything like this? Ethan says, "Please don't tell my mother. Please don't tell Emily."

xvii.

In the dithering circumstances, the idea of contacting Emily had not occurred to Elihu, but now that Ethan advances it, Elihu holds on to it for further contemplation.

Although Ethan is looking at Elihu for confirmation that he will not call his mother, Elihu says nothing, making a show of turning the tense discussion to immediate matters. "Right now we've got to get you out of the chair," he says, "and cleaned up. Later, we'll have plenty of time to talk about whatever we need to talk about."

He pushes the wastebasket aside and lifts Ethan from the chair. He receives little help from Ethan, who has not as yet regained much strength. Supporting Ethan as best he can, he awkwardly maneuvers the chair out of the way in order to get through the door and down the hall into the bathroom. This is not handily accomplished. Much stumbling ensues during the fifteen or so feet covered. Nothing is said, other than a few more swapped "I'm sorry"s.

In front of the shower stall, Elihu turns Ethan towards him and raises Ethan's arms so he can remove the splattered T-shirt. That completed, he turns Ethan around and lowers his boxers, helping Ethan raise one leg after the other to get out of them. Ethan has flat feet. He had not noticed that before. Elihu does not have flat feet. From whence would Ethan have acquired those?

He relishes none of this handling Ethan's body. He asks himself, "Is this what fathers are expected to do?" He doubts it comes to this extreme for most fathers. Is it his recompense for missing all the diaper changing? It's definitely something he vows he'll never do again.

"Can you shower yourself?" he says to Ethan, who allows some kind of non-verbal assent. Elihu thought to say and then not to say, "I'm not going to get in the shower with you."

Leaving Ethan to stand by himself—to steady an arm against a tiled wall, that is—Elihu opens the shower stall door and reaches in to adjust the faucets. He has the thought, a malevolent thought, to adjust to extremely hot water. As punishment? No, he mustn't. He can't. Whatever else this is, it's not the time to be punitive.

When the water reaches a proper temperature, Elihu says to Ethan, who still doesn't appear to be steady on his big feet, "You can get in now." Although tempted, he stops himself from giving any bathing instructions. He says, "I'll be right here if you need me."

While listening to the water running, watching steam billowing over the opaque shower-stall door to make the room misty, breathing the warming air and hearing the odd utterance Ethan issues, Elihu sits on the covered toilet seat and reviews the last half hour.

He shakes his head in belated disbelief. What's taken place is unbelievable, incredible, nothing he could ever have dreamed up in his former-fiction-writer's head. It's now that he remembers Ethan's plea that he not tell Emily. It comes to him that he wants to tell someone, to share this with someone, to unburden to someone this unexpected, unprepared for, unwanted turn of bizarre events.

Who else qualifies? No one. The boy's mother only. The other parent. From whom else could he elicit an explanation for what he has just gone through? Should he have seen it coming? Perhaps he should have. But no. There's no way he could have seen this coming. Or could he have? The abbreviated 9/11 Memorial jaunt comes to him. Ethan's curiously grave reaction to the site. Was that an omen? The increasingly long bedroom retreats, other omens? The night of the living drunk? Maybe they should have been. His aversion to "should" comes to him. Not a time for that, either. Ethan has been under his roof for going on five months. Writers are observers. Any writer worth his salt is able to connect big, fat dots. But, Elihu thinks, slowly shaking his head, he isn't worth his salt. He hasn't been for decades. Perhaps he never was.

His only recourse in this baffling hour is to contact Emily. He takes for granted that Ethan knows the information and also assumes that Ethan hasn't yet used it. He does not want to ask for it. There's another, almost as simple method. His lawyers not only have her address. They have her telephone number, a number he has never wanted. A cell phone number, no doubt.

He has never wanted to be in touch, not so much for his benefit but for hers. That's the way she has wanted it. Or is it the way he has wanted it? Or is it the way they both wanted it? It has been so long he doesn't know which is which, what's what. Sometimes when he thinks back on the affair, it seems as if it never happened. It seems a figment of his now withering imagination. A story he was told. Maybe a story he told himself for some unfathomable reason. For the plot of a novel he never wrote. He has indulged in this wayward conjecturing, despite the two hundred pounds of living proof showering three feet from him. Yes, he needs to consult Emily. For all he knows, the lawyers now have an email address for her. He does not want that. If he is going to alert her to this disagreeable incident, it cannot be by email. A phone call is bad enough.

He'll do it. Imminently. Right now, he hears the water turned off in the shower. He stands up to take a towel from the closet. He goes to the shower and calls into it. "Are you finished? Here's a towel." The door opens several inches. A wet and dripping forearm is extended up to the elbow. Elihu hands Ethan the towel. Ethan takes it and steps out. He is holding the towel in front of him.

"Are you all right now?" Elihu asks.

"I think so," Ethan says. He isn't looking at Elihu. His head is lowered. "I'm s—." He hesitates. "I'm so sorry. I don't know what…" He trails off.

Of course, he knows, Elihu says to himself. "We'll talk about it later," Elihu says. "Right now there are a few things I need to do." Elihu is thinking about the wastebasket and getting rid of its contents. "If I leave you alone for a few minutes, will you be all right?"

"I guess so, I think so," Ethan says. He is still holding the towel in front of him. There's something unspoken between them about a father seeing his son naked. Maybe in some families it's completely natural. It never was in Elihu's. He doesn't ever remember seeing Morris naked. Or Morris seeing him naked past his infancy. He does remember Jean remarking more than once in an annoyed tone that Morris rarely changed Elihu's diapers. He knows he didn't imagine any sort of similar scenes for Seth Levy or Sabe Levensohn. He never would have thought to. Perhaps he should have, but revisions are now completely out of the question.

"Okay then, I'm going," Elihu says and starts to leave. He stops at the door. Without turning back, he says, "If you need anything, just call. I'll be downstairs for just a few minutes." He still has not turned around. "Are you sure you're okay?"

"I'm okay," Ethan says. "I'll be all right by myself."

Elihu is not entirely convinced. Since Ethan arrived, he had seemed okay enough, if not a great deal more, and look what happened. Elihu pulls the bathroom door behind him. He does not close it. He leaves it open an inch or so. He yells into the bathroom. "Leave the door open, Ethan." Something occurs to him. "From now on you have to leave all doors open." He goes to Ethan's room to round up the empty bottles. He counts them—there are eleven—and throws them into the wastebasket.

He'll see to it all in the kitchen, and here he is, emptying a wastebasket of eleven bottles and a son's vomit. He is offended not only by the foul odor but by the imposition. Instead of contemplating Henry James's *Portrait of a Lady* after a third reading, he is scrubbing a soiled wastebasket with the detergent Mrs. Woolard likes. He's doing this even though, now that he thinks of it, he could have left the job for Ethan. Without reflecting on it, he chose not to. Why embarrass the deserving, undeserving boy further?

He finishes the wastebasket chore and judges it's time to go about contacting Emily. He walks to the foot of the stairs. He listens for anything happening above him. He hears movement. He climbs several of the lower few stairs. From there he can see that the door to Ethan's room is open and assumes Ethan is behind it.

He calls, "Ethan?"

"Yeah, yeah, I'm here."

"Just checking."

As long as he's in there with the door ajar, Elihu figures he has sufficient time to call his lawyers' office and obtain Emily's number. If Ethan comes downstairs, he will hear footsteps, flatfooted footsteps.

He goes to the kitchen phone. His lawyers' assistant, with whom he's spoken many times but never remembers his name, answers and puts him on hold. He returns and reads Elihu the number. Elihu writes it on the Post-it pad he keeps near the lone telephone and peels off the small sheet.

Just as he slips the note into a pocket, Ethan comes in. He's made no sound coming down the two flights of stairs. Somehow the two stairs that creak didn't—or they did and Elihu missed hearing them. Ethan is wearing his sweatshirt and baggy trousers. He has combed his hair, slicked it back. Its spring is temporarily tamed. If Elihu is right, Ethan has even slapped on some cologne. He is bare-footed. He looks as if he's made the attempt to look—and smell—fresh. This is new, Elihu thinks. "I used some of the deodorant you keep in the bathroom," Ethan says. "I hope you don't mind."

About deodorant, Ethan is now bothered.

"Sit down," Elihu says. "We need to talk." He points at the kitchen table and the empty chair beside it. Ethan sits. Elihu says, "What was that all about?"

Ethan says, affecting a hangdog expression that Elihu does not completely buy, "I don't know what to say."

"I'm sure you do know what to say, Ethan," Elihu says, "and I have a few things to say myself."

He waits for Ethan to say whatever it occurs to him to say. He even tips his head up as a cue. It's a cue to which Ethan—seated with the abashed expression continuing to fill his round face and with his fingers loosely holding the tabletop—doesn't respond.

Elihu decides not to wait. "You just tried to take your life, Ethan. Forget how inadequately. You probably would have slept it off, but I didn't want to take the chance. Why did you do it? I could ask why you chose to do it on *my* time, but I won't."

More than that, Elihu wants to say something very much on his mind—that Ethan's pathetic attempt has been, among other things, a provocation—but retreats from what he recognizes as continuing to make it as much about him as about Ethan. He's disturbed at that reaction while acknowledging to himself the truth of it. For the moment he will focus on Ethan. He will get back to the other aspect later.

"I'm waiting," Elihu says, and this time he is set on waiting as long as it takes.

Though not timing the wait—not glancing at the kitchen clock to watch the seconds turn—he gets the feeling he's waiting fifteen, twenty, at least thirty seconds before Ethan, clearly understanding he is expected to speak and just as clearly struggling to find words, finally says, but softly, "I don't have anything to live for."

Elihu hears the sentence. To begin with, he objects to the tone in which it's spoken. "What?" he demands, the anger he has been tamping down coming to the surface.

Ethan repeats himself, not loudly but at least louder, "I don't think I have anything to live for. What do I have to live for?"

Elihu recognizes the last phrase both is and isn't a rhetorical question. He guesses Ethan doesn't expect him to have a response. No, he suspects Ethan might expect Elihu to come up with an answer, an answer to which he then can say that's not a good enough reason. Elihu thinks he will answer but does not immediately know what he'll say. He decides to give himself time to conjure something from somewhere.

Ethan assumes a wry expression. "You see. You don't have anything to say."

"I could have something to say right off the bat," Elihu starts. "You know I could be glib and say you have everything to live for."

As he's speaking, he realizes he has the urge to take Ethan's hand, to grasp it to him—the gesture, he reasons to himself, adding weight to the sincerity he means to convey, the sincerity to which he's almost surprised he means to convey. He vaguely recalls having a similar hand-holding impulse on which he didn't act not that long before. He can't pinpoint when.

Maybe this time he should act on it. But when Elihu reaches over, Ethan—still grasping the table—drops both hands in his lap.

Elihu would like to believe he shows no reaction to Ethan's recoiling, but he's virtually certain the fleeting disappointment he feels crosses his face.

How he began the conversation stays with him, the somewhat mundane "What was that all about?" I'm talking to a boy—to a young man—whom I have fathered, he thinks. Is that what's behind his impulse to get through to Ethan? To get through to him, yes, but in what capacity? For the first time he's curious whether he is reacting as a father would to a son, or if he's talking to Ethan as he might talk to any acquaintance who had just done something drastic, something stupid, something pointless, something with seriously unknown repercussions. Which is it? As father or as concerned friend or even as unexpectedly involved stranger? More importantly, which ought it to be?

He doesn't know, but words are coming to him relating to not what just anyone has to live for but language applicable to Ethan specifically. Shouldn't words, the ideal language, come to, of all people, a writer? He's no longer a writer. In this unusual—no, not unusual, more like all-too-unforeseen—instance, he could give himself the benefit of the doubt and tell himself he is a writer who doesn't write. How regularly, how compulsively, he thinks, he reminds himself about his writer's status—that is, his former writer's status. Enough already.

But, writer or no longer writer, words for this occasion are now coming to him. "Look, Ethan," he says. Normally, he disdains people who begin sentences with "look" or "listen" or, worst of all, "well." He okays it this once, if only because in the circumstances it's helpfully demotic. "I can't tell you that you have everything to live for. I don't know you—."

"You got that right," Ethan says in rapid response. "You're my father—my biological father—." He puts "biological" in demeaning italics. He accompanies the word with as close to a sneer as he can get in his still compromised state. "—and that's the beginning of my not having anything to live for. I started life without a father. That's one of the first things you're supposed to have to live for. I'm not saying I missed things like tossing a baseball or a football around with the old man. Or my father showing me how to ride a bike."

Elihu wonders who did show Ethan how to ride a bike. Someone must have. A friend of the family? A male friend who was more than a friend? A stepfather? Fred? Mitchell? A man acting like a surrogate father? A woman? Emily?

Ethan is forging on. "Baseball, bikes, making model airplanes together? That's kid stuff. I mean things more basic than that. I'm talking about being wanted just as a son."

On that, Ethan pauses. Elihu sees Ethan going somewhere in his head. He is thinking something over. He finds what he's after and says, "I never thought of it that way, but that's part of what I mean. But only part of it. And don't tell me sending Emily a check every month counts for anything. It's just buying your way out of obligations."

When Ethan says that, spits it out—vomits it?—Elihu experiences what he has to think is an emotional elbowing of a sort he's never felt. He says, "That's not what I meant it to be."

"Too bad," Ethan says. "That's the way it felt. That's the way it feels."

Elihu tells from the unmodulated way Ethan is speaking, from the hard look in his black, somehow blacker, eyes, that to some extent—apparently to some large extent—here's the way his absence has taken its toll. He says and leans forward, "I did care about you. I wanted to make certain you would live comfortably. Your mother must have explained that."

"My mother? You don't even say her name."

"I haven't said her name?" Elihu asks, somewhat taken aback.

"Not once," Ethan says. "Not once."

Elihu thinks that over. He hasn't said her name. It's not that he doesn't think about her by name. He does. He thought of her earlier and used her name when asking for her phone number. But it's true he hasn't said her name to Ethan. It implies a familiarity he doesn't feel, that he's attempted not to feel, a familiarity that he doesn't want to remember. Why he doesn't want to remember it, to feel it, he can't name. No, it's a familiarity he doesn't want to name. That's it. That's *probably* it. But what is that *it*? Were he to identify it, he might have to admit to himself that he doesn't want to acknowledge Emily as someone he hasn't entirely resolved to put behind him. That can't be so. Or is his obstinate attitude towards those memories, towards that time, proof he's determined to put behind him something that he won't, or can't, put behind him fully, something never completely concluded? Proof that there's been no—abominable word coming—closure. No closure in *his* mind. Has there been in Emily's? Maybe not in hers, either.

After all, Emily and he share a son—Ethan. This prompts another thought, a thought it occurs to him he should have had much earlier. He says, "This foolish act you just pulled. Had you succeeded—which perhaps in some demented way you hoped you would—did you think about what it would do to your mother? The cruelty of it?"

Another question hits him. Did you think about what it would do to your father?

In any other situation the question would be just as obvious. He refrains from asking it. Who's the father to whom it would apply? To Fred whatever-his-name-is? To Mitchell Lombardo? Surely not to himself. What kind of a father has he been?

Elihu is thinking about this—and wondering whether the father query has also struck Ethan—while waiting for Ethan to respond to how he might have aggrieved Emily. Ethan isn't responding. So Elihu says,

"You have no answer for that. I'm not surprised. So like it or not, I'm calling her about this, about this—." He pauses to select the right word. "—about this incident."

He sees Ethan on the point of saying something, on the point of objecting. Is Ethan wondering if and/or how he's come by a phone number? If he has? He allows Ethan no opening but presses on. "It's decided. You don't have any say here. I'm calling her."

"I wish you wouldn't," Ethan says. "Please don't."

"I'm sorry," Elihu says with as much gravitas as he can muster, "you forfeited those rights."

"You don't know how to reach her," Ethan says, with satisfaction infusing his hangdog look. "You never call. You just send checks. I mean, you have checks sent. You don't even do that directly."

Elihu notices that the kitchen seems to have gotten warmer. Has he left the oven on? He looks around at the up-to-date oven with the flat burners he sometimes contemplates flattening a palm on merely to prove he's sentient. He hasn't left the oven on. Are the windows open? The door to the upstairs? Or is he imagining the warmth, the rising heat? Is it his own discomfort? Could be. He'll live with it. "I have your home number right here," he says, holding up the Post-it with the number on it.

Without really looking at the slip of paper, Ethan says, "That's the old number. It's been changed."

Elihu takes a split second to catch Ethan's attempt to stop him. "Nice try," he says. "It's the right number. I got it from my contact."

"That's just great," Ethan says. "You know about us through an unnamed, unspecified contact." He accompanies the "contact" with another quasi-sneer. "See what I mean? And you're telling me I have everything to live for."

"Don't put words in my mouth, Ethan. I expressly said I wouldn't insult you by saying you have everything to live for. You have a mother who loves you."

"But not a father."

"You have a home to go to. Look around. Apparently you have two homes to go to."

"Yeah? A rented home? And for how long? You're not going to throw me out after what I've just done?"

Elihu sees Ethan exerting himself more, as gradually he recovers from the past hour or so. He amends Ethan's feeble query, "After what you've just *not* done. Through ineptitude. Though it's lucky I happened into your room." He doesn't stop himself from amending himself. "Into the room. No. I'm not going to throw you out. Is that what you'd like me to do? To give you one more thing to feel bad about? Not by a long shot. I'm going to tell you you have a good brain. You've got your health. You're twenty-one"—he doesn't stop himself again and squeezes a little juice into it—"going on twenty-two any day now. You've got your whole life ahead of you."

Ethan raises his head and says—as if he's tapped into a moment of actual delight, which indicates to Elihu an intellectual promise he hadn't yet detected in the boy—"You're supposed to be a writer, and all you come up with is a remark that has whiskers on it? 'You've got your whole life ahead of you'? Is that any worse than 'I have nothing to live for'? I've got my whole life ahead of me? Yeah, and what's that life going to be? Nothing that amounts to anything, as far as I can tell."

Elihu remembers his anger. Ethan is giving him a hand with that. "Ethan, if you're looking to me for pity, you're not going to get it."

"I never got anything from you before. Why should I expect to get something now? Even if it's just pity. I don't want your pity, anyway. And another thing. About that music you've always got going. What is it?

Handel? Handel shmandel. It's making me nuts. Maybe that's the real reason I did what I did."

Elihu has had enough. "Handel shmandel!" Where did that come from? He'll find out another time. He holds up the phone number again for Ethan to see and speaks with defiance. (Here's a pulsating emotion he doesn't recall having experienced in some time. That's what this boy has brought out in him.) "I'm calling."

He goes to the wall phone and dials, looking directly at Ethan—deliberately not looking at the whitewashed walls or the pots hanging over the oven or Jean's cookbooks and the few others he's collected but hardly ever finds a reason to consult.

"It's ringing," he says, acknowledging to himself he didn't need to say that.

Ethan, subdued, resumes his hangdog, slope-shouldered look. Again, Elihu estimates Ethan's shoulders are as wide as, or even wider than, his. Waiting for the number to connect, Elihu also recalls his being asked to join Yale's freshman football team and declining, as he always had declined joining football teams when he was a husky kid. Butting helmeted heads was never for him, if it was for Ethan. In *Wandering Youth* Seth Levy does play football. It's another of the points on which Elihu always claimed the novel could not be considered autobiographical. "Seth Levy isn't me," he'd tell interviewers. "For one thing, I never played football. I was a swimmer. And only fair to middling, at the best of times."

Okay, so Ethan did play. If Elihu remembers in the next couple of days, he might get around to asking Ethan how good he was.

The phone is answered.

xviii.

When Emily Haas hears Elihu's voice, she recognizes it. This surprises Elihu but, he realizes, it shouldn't have. It was almost as if she expected a call, though likely not this particular call. She must have. "I knew Ethan was with you," she says. "When he said that since you never contact us, he would contact you, I didn't think it was such a good idea. I told him so. I mean, I wasn't sure it was a good idea, but he's twenty-one. He's old enough to make his own decisions."

Elihu cuts her off there. Addressing her point about age and independence, he says, "He wasn't twenty-one when he dropped out of Yale. Was he old enough to make that decision?"

Elihu never believed that coming of age is something that should be routinely conferred at twenty-one or eighteen or, for that matter, twenty-eight. He based it on his assessment of himself. He had definitely believed that he hadn't come of age—much as he would like to have—at thirteen by way of bar mitzvah. Most people would say the same about thirteen. He had even mooted the notion implicitly in *Wandering Youth*. Shmuel Garb, depicted as a frum Yid, says to Seth Levy, "Just because you're thirteen and own a fountain pen doesn't mean you're a mensch. It just means you're less of a pisher."

He is about to say something like that about Ethan, when Emily says, "Elihu, we haven't spoken in more than twenty years. Are we already having an argument? If I remember correctly, it would be our first."

Elihu would like to have known the answer to his question about Ethan's leaving Yale but hasn't the time to press for it. He has something to say that takes precedence. It also isn't that when he and Emily were together, she called him Eli. He has Ethan's sleeping-pills caper uppermost on this agenda and is determined he'll try to put the best face on what he's about to report. Assuming there could be a best face for it. Divulging the details as economically as he thinks fit, and deliberately leaving out the drinking bout that preceded it as too much to relay, he hears Emily's concern. He catches her mounting alarm.

When he has all but finished, she asks him to hold on and either puts her hand over the landline phone or perhaps holds a cell phone against her chest for a minute. Why the interruption? Does she need time to think? Is she consulting with someone else in the room? Her husband? Mitchell Lombardo? It must be. She speaks again. "Elihu, there was a time when it seemed as if you knew what I was thinking, and I knew what you were thinking. Maybe I still do. Is it a good idea for me to come out there? I think it is. If so, I will. I ought to. After all, he is my son. What I mean to say is, he is your son and my son. I can't really say 'our son.'"

The phone call ends shortly after that, Emily having said she would make the trip as quickly as she could.

Between the phone call and Emily's arrival the next day, the atmosphere in the house is subdued. Ethan leaves the bedroom door open when he's there. Uncertain about sleeping, Elihu occupies the second-floor back bedroom through the night, alternating between being aware of any sound he hears and dozing fitfully. When he awakens, he strips the bed to prepare it for Emily. While she's here, he will sleep in the library-study. He's aware that Ethan is stirring. He says, "Good morning, Ethan" sufficiently loudly for Ethan to hear him. He's greeted, if it can be called that, by a gruff "G'morning, Elihu."

One thing Elihu takes care of before getting breakfast for the two of them—Ethan's appetite seems unimpaired—is putting a stop to

Handel's *Concerti Grossi*. He notices, and this amuses him, that he is relieved at its ceasing. Ethan makes no mention of the new silence even when Elihu asks what kind of music Ethan likes listening to. "Whatever," Ethan says. Elihu has reached the point where he can tell that Ethan is feigning disinterest. He gives some thought to what he would like to pipe through the house and decides he'll do without for a while. He likes the relative quiet. More than that, he remembers that the *Concerti Grossi* were intended to drown out his thoughts. Now something else—someone else—is occupying them, and he mustn't ignore them.

Less than twenty-four generally uneventful hours later, a taxi pulls up in front of 73 East Ninth Street. Emily Haas gets out. She had called when she landed at LaGuardia. Elihu, reckoning on possible bad traffic into Manhattan, timed her arrival as closely as he could and is waiting for her at the top of the brownstone stoop. Ethan is with him. Elihu sees to that. For the most part, Ethan, who had found his tongue for a few remarks the day before, is cooperative. Now he's standing to the right and slightly behind Elihu. Not beside him. Elihu figures the boy is making some kind of point but lets it go.

The cab driver removes Emily's small valise from his trunk. Not much luggage, Elihu registers. Does this indicate she doesn't plan to stay long? What else could it mean? Surely, she isn't having a larger suitcase sent or, heaven forbid, a trunk. She has undoubtedly thought this through and, knowing Ethan as she does—as she has to—has calculated that only a short stay is necessary. Very likely for talking him into returning with her to Cleveland. If that's the case, Elihu is relieved for Ethan, for her and (most of all?) for himself.

Ethan, suddenly a good boy, brushes past Elihu, saying, "I'll get the valise, Emily." He hustles down the steps with an athleticism Elihu hasn't seen and, after the previous day, is not expecting. Oh, Elihu realizes, Ethan is making a disarming (calculated?) impression. Emily stops him for a hug. Elihu notes that it's an uneasy hug, which isn't entirely attributable to Ethan's girth in comparison with Emily's still slim figure. She's put on some weight, Elihu takes in, but not that much. Though Ethan's bulk diminishes Emily as would a bear embracing a recently planted tree, his burst of energy has evaporated. What looms between mother and son in the way of Ethan's bout of misconduct—misconduct is what it's shading into in Elihu's mind—now borders on palpable.

Also, Elihu is mindful that this is Emily Haas. This is the girl, the young woman, the student with whom he passed several (suddenly?) memorable months twenty-something years earlier, "memorable" not being a vague catchall but a memory loop playing in his head as he looks at the woman hugging the son for which he is in some ways as responsible as she is. Or is that a non-feminist attitude?

But who is Emily Haas now? She is older, of course. From the several feet away that she is, Elihu sees she has changed the way she wears her hair, her auburn hair, her still seemingly auburn hair. Where it had once hung to her shoulders, she has cropped it shorter, not short but shorter. From where he's standing he notices she has allowed some grey to invade. How like the Emily he remembers not to make a big deal about that. The late spring sun is shining on both mother and son, and, Emily facing him, it lights up the features Elihu realizes he knows well—the features he once knew well, the strong features he often watched in some amazement at himself, while she was sleeping next to him and he would lie on his side, head raised and resting on one hand.

Emily's face has aged over the twenty intervening years, but the soft June sun erases, as it always does, any indication of that—as opposed, Elihu thinks, to the often-unforgiving tricks played by the harsh winter sun. Emily has closed her eyes for the hug, but Elihu assumes they're still ice blue. He sees the full eyebrows, the straight nose he always liked, the curved mouth, the strong chin, the oval shaped face.

Looking at Emily after all this time, Elihu feels a pang he isn't able to index. It isn't love. He is positive of that. He did love Emily then, in perhaps a careless way, but he cannot remember whether he was truly in love with her. He is never certain he was in love with any of the women and the one man (Bart Norcross) he may have thought at the time he was in love with. He has always supposed that if, on looking back at an affair, he couldn't recall what being in love felt like, then he could not have been in love. That makes sense, doesn't it? It always has to him. It still does.

But what he's feeling at the moment must have meaning. Is it nostalgia? Nostalgia for what once was and can never be again? Does nostalgia manifest itself in faint sensations like the one he's unexpectedly undergoing? He's aware of his heart. Not pounding, merely beating. He's never aware of his beating heart, the heart he has, more often than not, figured for a muscle too habitually burdened with superfluous attributes.

It doesn't matter, Elihu concludes as he watches the mother-and-son reunion. The strain from a Paul Simon song sneaks into his head. What's it called? What *is* it? "The Mother and Child Reunion." That's it. It slid into his head as do many pop songs to which he isn't aware he ever paid much attention.

Is what he's feeling a recollection of love for Emily? It's not that, but it's enough that he recognizes he has some vestigial whatever-it-is for her. He knows that having anything approaching this feeling, these feelings, at the moment—unforeseen as of a day earlier—is an encouraging development. He can have feelings, he knows he needs to have them, he assures himself, but that doesn't mean he has to show them. He rates it a fair-enough compromise. He can save them for his writing. *Were* he writing.

Emily and Ethan complete their hug, and Emily begins to walk towards Elihu, who has remained at the top of the stoop. It behooves him to go to greet her. As he takes the stairs one at a time, he's briefly sidetracked into focusing on the many times he's gone up and down them by now—but only because that's the way any resident enters and leaves a place. For him that's the purpose stoops serve. He's never stood on them for anything like this unanticipated occasion. This is what other people—but not him—often use their steps for, neighbors with family and friends to greet and send off.

Evidently, it has just become his turn. He looks Emily over. She's wearing a lightweight pink blazer, loose grey slacks, grey flats, a filmy pink-and-grey scarf around her neck. Women approaching middle age often wear scarves to hide their necks. Does that explain this one? Has Emily tied it dashingly for his sake? Or is she just being generically stylish? When he knew her, she wore the same run of clothes around the University of Chicago campus that the other female students wore. In his estimation she always managed to look better in them. Flair. That's what she had. An intangible trait, but she had it—a sly combination of calculation and off-handedness. He remembered his landlady used to say that about her. Mrs. Brady didn't say "flair," but that's what she meant. Mrs. Brady. Her name was Mrs. Brady, Elihu thinks—Mrs. Frances Brady, if he remembers correctly. He hasn't thought of Mrs. Brady in years. Why would he have?

Tall, Elihu says to himself as, taking his measured time as the memories crowd him. Emily was always tall and proud of her height. Good posture. He had always admired that in her. Good posture, Jean had always said, is a positive sign. With Emily, it was a sign she knew who she was. That is, she knew who she was at the times when she didn't let slip in some unspoken way that she was still uncertain who she was. Elihu recalls that at times like those, he would think that what he had to say to her, quite often about her, could, would, influence who she was becoming.

He'd met her when she was still at an impressionable age. He met her, he notes, when she was about the same age Ethan is now.

He recalls something else he'd long since forgotten—that while taking pride (as he now judges it) in the effect he was having on her, she was having her effect on him. He suddenly remembers she had once insisted they go to a student concert where Handel's *Concerti Grossi* had been played. Students played it—students, who, as it happened, weren't majoring in music.

That's it. Of course, Elihu recalls. Emily was the one who brought the *Concerti Grossi* to his attention. Why had he not remembered it was she? Was it something he had unconsciously blocked? Should he reinstate them later in the day to see how she would react, what she would remember of their part in the shared past? No, this is no time for *old* times. Now he remembered that she had explained that the young concertizing musicians were majoring in other subjects but committed to continuing with their instruments. She knew two or three of them. So that's where the months-long spate of Handel's *Concerti Grossi* had come from. Talk about the way in which waning memories have their effect, he thinks and almost stops in his measured tracks down the steps.

He doesn't, and in those few seconds he sees that the Emily coming to meet him is the Emily who knows who she is or makes a good pretense of it. He takes four steps down, while she's climbing up. He's one step above her. She extends her hand, and he extends his. She changes her mind and opens her arms to hug him. He doesn't know what he's supposed to do. Now she doesn't, either. Just as he understands he should be a good sport and go in for the hug, she stops in mid-gesture, then understands she has no choice but to respond in kind. It's a hug they hold longer than they might have. That's to give themselves and each other the notion that the hug is not as uneasy as it is—Elihu leaning down so that his balance is in question, Emily craning up in a manner that could be straining her back. To cover their on-stoop inelegance further, they give in to nervous laughs.

"Elihu," Emily says as they end the threatening-to-be-endless embrace. He hears the "Elihu" as a premeditated distancing tactic.

They speak at the same time. The hellos, the good-to-see-yous, the it's-been-so-longs overlap and are followed by a silence during which each waits for the other to speak. Instead, Ethan, hurrying past them with Emily's valise, says, "Are you guys coming inside?"

Elihu gestures for Emily to precede him. She does, and they follow Ethan. In the hall, Ethan puts Emily's valise down and asks Elihu what he should do with it. Should he take it upstairs? He knows that his mother will be staying in the second-floor back bedroom. Elihu made a point of telling him. He did not say that it's really the only room for her, nor did he say that with his mother in the next room, Ethan isn't likely to repeat the recent tomfoolery. Elihu is counting on that.

Emily looks around and compliments Elihu on the house but then says with dispatch to Ethan, "The valise can wait. For the time being, we'll skip the other amenities, too. This is no casual visit, Ethan. We'd better get right down to brass tacks." She turns to Elihu. "Don't you think I'm right, Elihu?" Again, it strikes Elihu that he was Eli to her during the Chicago years—the Chicago half year. The "Elihu" is in recognition of their now quite different relationship.

Elihu starts to answer, but Emily isn't waiting for it. She looks around, peers into the front parlor and says, "What about the living room?" She doesn't wait for an answer but strides into the room with undiminished purpose. She turns around to make certain that Elihu and Ethan are following her. They are, with Elihu indicating to Ethan that he should track Emily and not lag behind as he looks about to be doing. It occurs to Elihu that in the past twenty-four hours, he has had to direct an excessive amount of traffic.

In the room, Emily goes to a wing chair Elihu has hauled along to many, though hardly all, of the houses and apartments and flats and maisons and cottages and casas and manors and the actual castle in south France he's inhabited during the last thirty or so years. The wing chair was his mother's—his father's, too, but really his mother's. It was Jean who chose the furnishings in the Trenton home where he grew up and where Morris was simply glad he didn't have to bother with women's work. Morris was content to mind the store. Sufficiently content was more like it.

Elihu sits not on anything inherited but on a long burgundy couch he found in an Upper East Side thrift shop and had delivered the same day. It suits the room well enough. He put it there with a couple side chairs and a circular table so that when he looks into the room, it does not appear empty. It's not a room he has expected to occupy often. On the other hand, he didn't want it to look desolate whenever he glanced at it. Desolation is anathema to him, because, he's loath to admit to himself, he doesn't want to have any suspicion that he is desolate confirmed to him *by* him.

He is *not* desolate. Ethan is the one giving off desolation signals.

Ethan sits on the upholstered chair between the parlor windows, the one Elihu sized up when he first entered 73 East Ninth Street. He had wondered then whether he would ever sit on it. So far he hasn't. Neither has anyone else until now. Had Mrs. Woolard sneaked a break on the chair? He doubts it. He's never observed Mrs. Woolard being anything but industrious, being anything but seriously conscientious about her work.

Something comes to Elihu. He says, "Emily, you've just arrived. Do you want anything? Something to drink? Before we start talking?"

She gives him a fleeting smile—the curved lips he remembers—and says, "Later. Right now I want to know what's going on here. What went on here. Your turn, Ethan."

Elihu turns to Ethan, which is what he should do, but he's thinking about Emily. She is no longer the graduating twenty-two-year-old student with whom he was romantically involved, with whom he was gladly, even eagerly, entangled, but by whom he was never overwhelmed, near as he knows. It was a lovely fling, he unreservedly concedes to himself.

Now she's someone different. She's a mother in her forties. And what kind of mother? At the moment, she's giving evidence that she's a mother who brooks no foolhardiness from a son. But short of a mother who had little interest in her children at all, what mother wouldn't want to find out everything that had led to an attempted suicide? No matter how foiled it was. No, this isn't the Emily he knew, but somewhere in her has to be much remaining of the young Emily he did know. This Emily looks enough like her. Many of her expressions are the same. Just now with her challenging Ethan, she displayed familiar ones she had affected when chiding him over a small breach or when calling him on a social infringement about which she contended he should have known better.

Thinking that, he senses he's about to smile. Not a good idea. He should be waiting for Ethan to speak. He should assume a neutral manner, a manner devoid of any sort of giveaway look while the seconds are edging by.

Ethan, as if abruptly intrigued by the pattern in the flea-market throw rug Elihu picked up, finally says, "I don't know what to say, Mom."

"Don't give me that, Ethan," Emily says. She's leaning forward from the wing chair with her hands clasped on her lap. It's a pose Elihu remembers but also remembers that when, twenty-two years or so earlier, she struck that pose, her hair, that auburn hair, would fall forward, partially obscuring her face. At those times, Elihu recalls, she could be at her most seductive, her sexiest. Maybe she cropped her hair in deference to no longer being that young woman.

"Ethan," Emily says with a tone nearly insinuating menace, "you know exactly what you need to say. What made you do such a stupid thing? Stockpiling Melatonin. Ethan. What were you thinking?"

With a hell of a hangdog expression, Ethan says, "I guess I wasn't thinking."

Emily went on, "I'm tempted to say what everybody says in situations like this, that you were—are—calling for help. I'll say it. It may be a tired-out cliché, but we all know clichés are based on truth. So you made your call. I'm here answering it. Elihu is here, too, and as far as I can tell, there's no house cat to get your tongue. So speak up."

"Okay, Mom," Ethan starts. Elihu notices it's the second time Ethan has called Emily "Mom" and not Emily. What's the unwritten law governing when a boy brandishes rebellion, no matter how mild or wild, and when he refrains? Maybe it's the difference between deference and challenge? "You know how unhappy I've been. For a long time."

"I know that," Emily says. "That's what you always say to cut off any discussion. I wish you would look at me when you're speaking to me. Not at the floor. What I don't know is *why* you're unhappy. You will never tell me. That's behind my not saying anything when you left to come here, as I think you knew I knew you would. Seeking an answer from—." She pauses for a split second, then says, "—from Elihu."

Elihu assumes all three of them know she was contemplating saying "from your father."

"I don't know what's gotten into me," Ethan says, raising his voice in frustration. "For so long now. I don't. If I knew, I'd tell you."

Elihu thinks to repeat Ethan's telling him about having nothing to live for. He decides not to. It's not his turn. He suspects it won't be his turn for a while. He'd had his turn for the past couple of months and had not taken it. He muffed it.

"You always say that," Emily replies, "but I think you do know. Or have some idea. Tell me." Here, she doesn't change her position other than to turn her head and look at Elihu, pointedly including him. "Tell us."

Elihu thinks this is not the Emily he knew. He knew a single young woman with a good head on her shoulders and ambitions she never articulated, because, he had thought back then, she couldn't articulate to herself what she hadn't yet decided. Now she's a mother. She had to become a different person. No, she didn't have to become a different person. People don't have to become different. In Elihu's estimation it's the rare individual who chooses to. Emily, he surmises, chose to.

Whereas he, Elihu thinks, chose not to become a different person. When he learned Emily was pregnant, he could have married her. Had he long ago argued for that, there's a good chance he'd have prevailed. He could have raised Ethan with her, but that's not who he was then, and that's not who he *chose* to become. His choosing to marry Emily, he reminded himself, and raise the son or daughter with her is not what she wanted, either.

Recalling that, a thought streaks across Elihu's mind he'd never had before. At the time he took it for granted that Emily knew him well enough to know how determined he was not to settle down. It wasn't for him. She wouldn't infringe on his resolute freedom.

But that wasn't all. He remembered she had sized him, had measured Elihu—Eli then—up and down and decided he was not good husband material. And does it follow, not good father material? As others had decided before and have since. Even at twenty-two she had to have been thinking that, as a single mother, she would be better off raising a child by herself or with her accepting parents or—even this!—falling in love with a man eager to bring up a child, even if he was not the biological father? She must have resolved something along those lines.

Not a far-fetched notion? Listening to things transpiring in a room so quiet Elihu all but thinks the air could be heard, he has to accept Emily was right. At forty-two he was obdurately cold to the idea of bringing up a child. Nothing had altered in the intervening years. He had never been a young man like others he knew, like two of his Yale roommates, Randy Schmidt and Ike Rieber. They couldn't wait to get married and have kids. It sometimes seemed it's all they talked about. With Elihu as one of the six groomsmen, Randy married Candy Hodges the day after graduation. They were Randy and Candy, a rhyming couple, just the sort who ought to be parents, Elihu said then and not just to himself. He even said as much to friends at the Randy-rhymes-with-Candy reception with the loquacious purpose of reaping, he thought then, nothing more than cheap laughs. Now he hears something else in his snide remark: mockery of an institution he wanted to disparage entirely.

Neither husband material nor father material was the Eli of shortest, gladdest college years—or, he heartily reconfirms to himself, is the Elihu of the present moment. If that's what Emily had been thinking, Elihu has to agree. The events of the last day seem to bear that out.

But Ethan, looking like a little Buddha as he sits on the finally occupied chair Elihu inherited from the previous tenant(s), is speaking. Having started slowly, he's accelerating at a steady pace. "I just don't have any ambition, Mom. You know that. There's nothing I've ever wanted to do. Not for any length of time. Sure, when I was a kid, I wanted to be a fireman or a lineman on the Cleveland Browns, but I was never good enough for that. Nowhere near." Yes, Ethan had played football, according to many standard childhood ambitions. Elihu knows the photograph. "I wanted to be Superman. Remember that Halloween? All kids want that stuff. But when you get older and have to face reality, nothing interested me enough. That's why I dropped out of Yale. College is supposed to prepare you for something. I was in my junior year—April of my junior year—and I was preparing for nothing. Was I going to go to law school or medical school or hop on the track to Wall Street like all the other losers? *Please*. I wasn't going to be a writer, either, and write bestsellers. Like Elihu." Ethan tilts his head towards Elihu but doesn't look at him. "So I thought I'd drift around and find myself. Find myself." With his thick fingers, Ethan puts the two words in air quotes. "'Find myself.' What a dumb phrase. I wasn't going to find myself. I never had a real self to find. I never even had a self to lose. Not a self I liked much or knew much about.

"Not that I didn't try to figure something out, figure *some*one out. I attempted to with Doctor Emmons, but I just resented him. Half the time I'd just look at him and say nothing. He knew my story, though. He knew enough of it. More than once he asked me how I felt about—how I felt about all sorts of things—and over and over how I felt about growing up without a father. 'As if I ever thought about it,' I'd say. He kept saying I had to think about it sometime. He said I had friends with fathers. How did I feel about that? I'd say I had two stepfathers. Not the same thing, he'd go. I'd tell him so many of my friends had divorced parents where the fathers were the ones who moved out of the house that not having a father was practically the going state of affairs. Then I'd repeat the same thing. Maybe it was snotty. I don't know. I'd say, 'You can't miss what you never had.'"

When Ethan says that, he looks at Elihu with an expression Elihu can't begin to fathom. Is it insulting? Is it accusatory? Dismissive? When Ethan finishes the facial aside, he turns back to Emily. "But then I started thinking it over. Maybe you can miss what you never had." He focuses on Emily. "You figured that out when I started asking questions about him. You knew I was wondering what it would be like to have a real father around, what he might be like. I know you knew I did."

Now Ethan shifts to Elihu, and it's as if he's examining a specimen. Maybe I *am* a specimen, Elihu thinks. He hears himself saying to himself, another common species: the absent father. The next related thought Elihu has is something he hates admitting under any circumstance: I'm a statistic, an absent-father statistic.

"And I thought, what if I meet him?" Ethan is saying. "Will that make a difference? Well, I told you about that. I know I did." Emily nods assent. "I thought maybe I just have a hole in my—in my I don't know what—a hole in my psyche that needs to be filled in."

Elihu lets the irritating "well" slide. Why is he glomming on to a "well" when something of far more import is transpiring? What does that say about his unbridled avoidance impulse?

Emily says to Ethan, "Yes, you did tell me. I didn't agree with you when you said it, but you did say it. More than once."

Ethan says, "At first I didn't think it was a good thing to do, either. Then I thought, why not? What else am I doing that's so important? I'm letting you support me. And Mitchell. And those checks you told me about. Why not crash with my real father for a while and see what that gets me, see if I can figure anything out? I'm sorry I left without telling you where I was going, but I knew you'd figure it out. You always do."

"Does that bother you?" Emily asks.

"Yeah, Doctor Emmons," Ethan springs back with. "I guess it does. When you never called to see how I was doing, what I was doing, I figured you had figured it out and were just letting me find myself."

Ethan puts the "find myself" into more air quotes. "That's why I never bothered to call you. Or text. Why bother to tell you something you already knew?"

Elihu thinks there's something off-kilter about Emily's assuming what Ethan was up to. She couldn't be certain, and if not, why not put in at least one warning call Elihu's way, or, if not that, an eventual substantiating call? His lawyers always have his number. Not email address. For years he's wanted no email address. He says nothing. It's still not his turn.

"You thought that through correctly," Emily says. She changes her position, leans back without relaxing her close scrutiny of Ethan. "But maybe in light of what's happened I should have called you or Elihu. I kept thinking maybe the two of you needed some father-son space for the first time in both your lives." She took a moment to look at Elihu, then back at Ethan, then at Elihu again and held the gaze. "Maybe it was time I stepped aside for a while. Maybe I shouldn't have."

"Yeah, no, what you did was right, I guess," Ethan says. Elihu notes the second "I guess" in as many minutes. He wonders if the myriad "I guess"es annoy Emily as much as they do him. Then he thinks that at least Ethan hasn't gotten into the habit of dropping the word "like" three or four times into sentence after sentence, as everyone else in his generation does. Elihu cannot walk down a Manhattan street without hearing proliferating "like"s and having to stop himself from butting in with a cutting remark. He wonders if Ethan had acquired the "like" habit but had it drummed out of him by Emily.

Now he catches himself worrying about the use of "like."

"How right can it have been for me to let you go with so little discussion?" Emily is asking. "Here I am on an emergency trip, and it hasn't surprised Mitchell. He knew what was happening but for the most part kept out of it. But after no more than a week he suggested I—we—hire a private detective to follow you. I didn't think it was necessary. The weeks before you left, you'd asked more questions about your father than you ever had. I was sure, but Mitchell pressed me. 'Why not make sure?' He had a point. So we hired one and emailed him a photograph. It didn't take days for him to get back to us to confirm you were seen going in and out of 73 East Ninth Street in Manhattan."

Ethan, startled, says, "You did? I never saw any detective hanging around." He turns to Elihu. "Did you?"

Elihu says, "No, but I wasn't looking."

Emily says, "When you have a good one, you don't see him hanging around. He wasn't cheap, either. And even after that, I was having second thoughts about letting you come here."

For a second Ethan looks at Emily and then lets pass whatever he was thinking to say. Instead, "Maybe you shouldn't of. Something hasn't really gone right. What I found out is that staying with a father who is and isn't a father hasn't explained anything to me. I found out that I was nuts to think that if I got to know him—got to know Elihu—everything would click into place. If nothing in my life has ever clicked into place, what's the point of fooling myself into thinking it ever would? I'm not blaming Elihu." Ethan still doesn't look at Elihu. "He's been okay. I mean, he took me in. He gave me a room. He gave me a roof over my head, which I guess fathers are supposed to do. He's fed me. That's nice, but if you ask me, I'm a boarder here. Most days we're like ships that pass in the night."

Elihu chides himself for registering the mixed metaphors.

When Ethan finishes emitting them, he pounds his left hand into his right palm. The sound reverberates. "Listen to me. 'Ships that pass in the night.' If that's all I can come up with, that alone is enough to make me want to commit suicide."

Emily breaks in. "That's not funny, Ethan. We're not ready to hear jokes on the subject."

"Maybe me joking about it shows I'm over it," Ethan shoots back.

"Are you?" Emily asks.

"I dunno," Ethan says. He's shaking his head slowly.

"You better know," Emily says.

"I know I'm over the drinking," Ethan says, letting an expression form that signals he realizes what he's let slip and simultaneously gets that there's nothing he can do about it now.

"The drinking," Emily says in a chilled matter-of-fact tone.

Elihu experiences an unexpected, even protective, urge. "He came home drunk one night. Not that drunk. High. What Yale man doesn't at least once in his life?" Why pile Pelion on Ossa, Elihu asks himself, at this fragile moment?

Ethan also is unprepared for this. Elihu catches him blinking but saying nothing. He sees Emily chose to let it pass. Instead, she asks, "Where do you stand on all of this?"

So now it's his turn in the interrogation. She waits for an answer. So does Ethan, whom Elihu sees looking at him with relief and with, he thinks he detects, something of the rascal in his now rapt attention.

"Where do you think I stand?" Elihu says, having so hastily been snatched from his auditor position. "I'm not in favor of someone choosing my house as the place to take his life. To try to take his life."

"Not just someone," Emily corrects. "Your son."

"I'm his son in name only," Ethan says. "Not even in name only. I don't have his name," he continues, aiming full attention on Emily. "I have your name. I'm Ethan Haas. I'm not Ethan Goulding."

This is something about which Elihu hasn't thought. He's acknowledged to himself that Ethan is a son of his but he's held off regarding himself as an actual father. Would he feel different had a twenty-one-year-old Ethan Goulding arrived at his rented forest-green door? He doesn't think so, but he doesn't know. A son. Ethan Goulding. He actually does like the sound of it. It isn't Handel, but it has a musical ring for him.

"You have my name, because I wanted you to have it," Emily says. "Perhaps I never told you. It was not Elihu's—Eli's—choice. I presented it to him." To Elihu she says, "I did, didn't I?"

She must mean, Elihu thinks, the birth announcement.

Not waiting for an answer, Emily says to Ethan, "When I realized I was pregnant and wanted to have the baby—when I realized I wanted to have you—I didn't consider Elihu part of the decision."

When Emily interjects "when I realized I wanted to have you," Elihu hears the clearly explicit wording as unconsciously maternal, as naturally maternal. The feeling accompanying his analysis is—he's surprised at himself—close to moving. It *is* moving.

Ethan says, abruptly, to Emily, "You mean, you wanted me. He didn't."

Elihu rankles at the "he" and wonders why he did. The statement is, for all intents, true.

"I've explained this to you," Emily says. "It didn't matter what Elihu wanted or didn't want. I never asked. It was what I wanted. I was steeped in feminist think. I still am. I believed then, as I do now, that the decision was totally mine. Possibly I would have included Eli—he was Eli to me then—in my figuring had I believed he was in the marriage-and-children mood. Mode. I may have only been twenty-two, but I knew he was not."

"So you didn't want me," Ethan accuses Elihu. "You didn't want me to be born."

Elihu says, "That isn't it at all. I wanted for Emily—for your mother—I wanted for her to have whatever she wanted for herself. She was right. I loved her. I was in love with her." Whether he was or wasn't,

Elihu thinks, isn't pertinent. What is pertinent is to say he was. "But I was who I was then. I wasn't the marrying kind. I don't know why, but I just wasn't, son."

Elihu hears the "son" and is incredulous. He looks first at Emily and then at Ethan. Where did that come from? From wherever it catapulted, he cannot take it back. He can't unsay it no matter how much he wants to. Does he want to? And, really, how did he mean "son"? How had he meant it when it shot forth like a silver bullet? Had he intended it not in the personal sense but in the generic? Undoubtedly he meant it, he tries to convince himself, as the "son" a man might use when speaking politely to any younger male. He must have meant it—wants to have meant it—as not carrying any suggestion of parental possession, of parental supervision.

Emily and Ethan are reacting to the "son," too—but by acting as if they had not heard the immensely charged word. That is, neither says anything. In a way, they know they don't have to. There is silence, but their faces say plenty—or enough to tell Elihu they've taken the "son" in. They comment on it jointly by not commenting.

Nevertheless, Emily is looking at Elihu with her lips curved to say something like, I knew it all along. Despite everything he's insisted about himself he has this in him.

Elihu accepts the unspoken sentences he's convinced Emily is holding back—the reticence behind what's unspoken—as her deciding that were she to speak then, it would be premature and possibly cause Elihu to retreat from a newly revealed truth.

Ethan's expression discloses something different. In his dark eyes is a not-yet-trusted glimmer of hope. Whereas Emily's oval face reveals a satisfied confidence, Ethan's discloses uncertainty. Has he secured himself a father, a father whom he may not even like but a father all the same, a father who now might offer him he doesn't know what but something?

The silence that takes hold after Elihu's last remark is prolonging, as are the held gazes. Emily ceases hers with a slight shake of her head. She says, "Perhaps we've all said enough for the time being. Maybe it's a good idea to think things over. I wouldn't mind seeing the room where I'm staying."

Elihu and Ethan both get up. Emily looks at them, one then the other, then at each again and says to Elihu, "Just tell me which room is mine, and I'll find it on my own." She looks at her watch. "It's nearly five. We're going to have to do something about dinner. Since I haven't come here to cook, maybe Elihu can or Ethan can or maybe we can all go out for something. This is Manhattan. There must be a good restaurant close by. Why don't we get together at six and decide? In the meantime, maybe you two can talk. Or not."

Elihu doesn't know about Ethan and him talking. He says, "You're in the back bedroom on the second floor. It's ready for you."

"Very domestic, Eli," Emily says as she's turning. "That's new." Without looking at either Elihu or Ethan, she goes to leave the room but stops at the door. "One last thing," she says, and looks at Ethan. "Tell me this, Ethan. When you decided to go through with this, when you were taking those pills, did you give any thought to how I would be affected? Your mother?" When she demands this, Elihu thinks he detects the slightest catch in her voice. But if so, she doesn't indicate she's noticed. Instead, she says, "Did you give any thought to how your father would be affected?"

When she asks the second question, she does look at Elihu but for only a second. She switches her attention again to Ethan. She shoots him another of her penetrating gazes but doesn't wait for an answer. She only says, "Think that over" and leaves the room.

In a few seconds, Elihu hears her steps on the staircase.

He and Ethan look at each other but don't say anything. Elihu isn't ready to say anything more. He knows he's not prepared to invoke another "son." He mutters, "How about we do what your mother says—meet down here at six."

Ethan mutters something in response. It's not clear to Elihu, but he gets the gist. Ethan is just as eager to escape as he is. Something has changed, something intangible, about which neither is certain. Better to let it rest for the moment.

They both go upstairs without saying anything. Ethan goes into his room. Elihu is ready to yield that for the time being—however long that is—the room is Ethan's. At last the "his" applies. When he passes the second bedroom, he sees that Emily has shut the door. He thinks about listening at the closed door. For what? He checks himself and walks up to the third floor, to the library-study and the two convertible beds installed there. He doesn't close either of the two doors leading into it. Trying to concentrate on nothing—certainly not the word "son" and its myriad dangerous connotations in his life—he goes about getting ready for six o'clock.

xix.

When Elihu, Emily and Ethan meet in the parlor for their proposed meal, they decide to eat out. Not at Gene's, but at one of the other restaurants where the dark corners are sufficiently obscuring. Elihu settles on Il Buona Tavola because he wonders what it would be like to eat again with Emily at a neighborhood Italian restaurant. He wants to see whether the very arrival of straw-encased Chianti will provoke memories in her, whether the red-and-white tablecloths will trigger even a brief reference to the Chicago days, whether a waiter with an Italian accent will stir some mention of distant enchanted evenings. Had there been photographs of one or more of those times, he muses, they would have acquired the effect of more innocent times common to images from earlier years, common to fading images from receding decades.

On the short walk to Il Buona Tavola, Emily does not go near any kind of reminiscence. She continues in the vein of the earlier discussion but not directly on the core event. She wants to hear from Ethan what he has learned about New York, where he's gone, what he's done. Elihu recognizes the matter-of-fact practicality she exhibited when she was twenty-two, a personality facet now evolved into motherly concerns. She is a mother trying to determine whether her apparently unmoored son has made any beneficial use of his entirely free time.

When they arrive at Il Buona Tavola, Emily takes in the typical Italian restaurant surroundings. She takes in the waiter and the menu that doesn't deviate in any significant way from neighborhood Italian restaurants anywhere. She has no comment on them. For all Elihu can ascertain, she might have altogether forgotten their Italian restaurant past. For all he knew, she has intentionally put it out of her mind.

Elihu thinks of making some offhanded remark. He might say conversationally—jovially—something like, "Does this bring back anything, Emily?" Waving his arm casually at the room lighted only by candles dripping wax over fat-bellied bottles, he might say, "Previous outings?" He decides against it. It would be leading her, and he doesn't want to do that. For one thing, she may not want to be reminded of an affair she had twenty-years-plus earlier, an affair she had before a marriage and then a divorce and a second marriage. She might dismiss him with a disinterested couple of words. Then where would he be?

When they've ordered, Emily changes her manner. She indulges in small talk. She asks how Elihu found the East Ninth Street house. She knows he's peripatetic. She uses the word. She asks about where he has been living in the past few years. She doesn't know because the checks she receives, which she doesn't mention, always come from the lawyers' office. She doesn't ask if he's been writing or thinking of returning to writing. She knows better. She remembers, it seems clear to Elihu, how annoyed he got—"hot under the collar" is the expression she once used to describe his annoyance—when college friends to whom she introduced him, some of them Goulding readers, asked what he was writing at the moment. His stock answer, which he realizes he has not had to reprise in years, was, "Thanks for asking, but I make a point of never talking about what I'm working on." It was futile to say he no longer wrote. That only extended the infringement on his time and his short temper. She says she is still in regular touch with her roommate Joyce, whom Elihu "must remember," and who's married to a psychoanalyst and living in Indianapolis. She adds that she lost track of roommate Jennifer soon after they graduated.

As Emily keeps up the banter, Elihu recognizes aspects of the Emily he knew. He recognizes her strategy when she understood that his mind was elsewhere, that he had left the conversation to ruminate about something completely other. He always appreciated her at it. It meant she was allowing him the chance to respond with the random "That sounds interesting" or "Oh, yes?" or "Is that so?" indicating he was listening to the conversation when she knew he wasn't.

As the waiter with Il Buona Tavola's Italian accent delivers the entrées, Emily turns her attention to Ethan. She says she's disappointed in his action and responds to his sinking shoulders by saying she doesn't intend to inquire any further about the episode itself but is "intrigued" about the thinking that led to it. Elihu thinks her use of "intrigued" is clever in the way it implies she's framing the suicide attempt as an adventure worth hearing about, as if slides could accompany whatever answers he gives.

This is a change from her earlier confrontation. Alternating asking about Ethan's New York City sojourns, she wants to know whether in Ethan's losing debate with himself over what he concluded was his unpromising existence he had weighed any positives against the evidently overwhelming negatives. She reminds him he has a good brain. Getting into Yale was an achievement, she points out, without being able to rely on any legacy—his surname being Haas, not Goulding—but only on his own abilities, his high school and SAT grades, obtained without his caring one way or another about them, as he'd repeatedly told her. She reminds him she never bought the claims, that she's always suspected he "cared more than he cared to admit"—as if copping to his interests would embarrass him were he to fall below a certain level.

When Emily presses Ethan on this aspect of his schooling, Elihu backs up against a *déjà vu* he knows well. He remembers Emily, younger and at times reticent but perceptive, asking him why he wasn't writing. This was in the early days of their courtship, before she understood that he meant it when he insisted he wanted the subject permanently dropped. Until then, he remembers her pressing him to explain why he had stopped, reiterating her disbelief that he didn't have anything in mind to write about.

Nowhere in what she's asking Ethan does he detect her speaking to him as well. She hasn't looked at him during her quizzing. It's more that she's intent on forcing Ethan to concede that somewhere in him he harbors interests on which he can build, as she had once implied Elihu must have harbored interests about which he could write.

Emily says to Ethan, "This afternoon you said you left Yale because it prepared you for nothing. You've said it before, but it just occurs to me there is another perspective. Couldn't you think of Yale as—this may sound corny—as a banquet with a buffet table from which you can put whatever you want on your plate? Just enjoy the—oh, I don't know—the dishes you like? This never occurred to me before. You might trust that somewhere in the choices you make, you'll eventually identify something you want to explore further."

Throughout Emily's discourse, Ethan sits quietly, giving nothing away, his arms on either side of his bowl when he isn't eating from it. Now he speaks, "That isn't how college works, Emily. You know that. I was in my junior year, when I should have already declared a major, and I had no idea what I wanted. Was I going to choose something—physics, English lit, political science—just for the hell of it? I don't think so. I wasn't interested in any of it. Interested enough. Okay, so I went for English lit. You know why? Because it sounded like the easiest. Maybe it was, maybe it wasn't. It just didn't matter to me—all that reading, all that talking about it." He turns to Elihu. "No offense, Elihu."

Elihu says nothing.

"So you drop out?" Emily asks. "That's your only alternative?"

"What other alternative did I have, besides closing my eyes and pointing at something else?"

"Aren't there faculty advisors, anyone you could go to and explain your dilemma? I know that may not be standard practice at colleges. But Yale? Isn't it supposed to be flexible? If a student presents a good enough argument why he or she would like to go differently about heading to a degree, might they listen to you at least? Did you try that?"

"I didn't think of it," Ethan says. "I told you that before, but even if I did, I wouldn't expect anything to come of it. Life isn't like that."

"You wouldn't even consider giving it a try?"

Ethan stops to evaluate this new strategy. It looks as if Emily has gotten through to him. Elihu sees something bordering on a gleam come into Ethan's eyes. Ethan says, "That could be kind of fun, doing that. A lot of these policies are Yale sitting on its high horse. I wouldn't mind trying to knock them off." He thinks this over, too. "But to do it, I'd have to go back."

Emily says, "But you know you can go back. Students drop out all the time for all sorts of reasons and then go back."

"But if I go back, even if they meet me half-way or something, I'd have to go back to classes. I'd have to pick something I like. What am I going to pick? Whatever they're picking now? Gender studies? There's nothing wrong with it. It's just not for me."

Elihu is following this and decides to put in his two cents. "There has to be something you like." In his mind he hears himself saying, "There has to be something you like, son," but he also hears himself having just said the sentence aloud without the "son." That's a relief. He adds only, "Something appealing?"

"Maybe English again," Ethan says. "I guess I like English, after all, and I was reading by the time I was three."

Three? Elihu remembers he didn't read until he was four, but he had Jean's influence. Ethan had Emily's. Jean only read to him occasionally. She left him to his own devices. There's even a passage in *Wandering Youth* where Seth asks his mother to read to him, and she tells him he's learned enough about the letters and words to figure it all out for himself. Elihu assumes that Emily would have made a habit of reading to Ethan.

Elihu also thinks that, given Ethan's enigmatic expression just then, his saying he was "reading by the time I was three" might be a joke, although he hadn't done much joking since he arrived. Elihu doesn't think he'll point it out. That might shut Ethan up.

Emily doesn't refer to Ethan's comment, either. She says, "Then there's something to go on."

"*If* I decide I want to go back," Ethan says. "I didn't say I would. Think of all the drawbacks. I'd be a couple of years older than my classmates. Not that that would be a big problem. I wasn't that crazy about the classmates I had. I guess they were all right."

Emily says, "You don't have to decide this minute. Why don't you sleep on it?" The subject is closed.

They finish dinner and return to the house in relative tranquility. Elihu notices that once in a while Emily gives Ethan a sidelong glance. She's sizing him up. She's looking for signs of his reconsidering the action that has her here.

Elihu is doing the same.

Emily suggests they all go to bed and resume talking at breakfast. "I said I'm not here to cook, and since this isn't my kitchen, I don't know where anything is. Ethan, how about you make breakfast?" She says to Elihu, "Has he made breakfast for you? He's good at it."

Ethan says, "I haven't done any cooking."

"Why not?"

"Elihu hasn't asked. It's his house."

"You've been staying here how long," Emily says, "and you haven't offered?"

"Well," Ethan says, noticeably crestfallen, "no."

"That settles it," Emily says to him. "Tomorrow morning you make breakfast," then to Elihu, "You're in for a surprise. Ethan's a good cook. I've seen to that."

"I'm okay," Ethan says to Elihu. "Don't get your hopes up too high."

Elihu says, "Why not let me be the judge of that?"

With only a few more amenities, they all retreat to their separate bedrooms.

Elihu hears the doors shut as he climbs to the third floor. It's only just past ten. He's not ready for bed yet. He takes off his shoes and goes to the club chair, next to which Ernest Hemingway's *A Farewell to Arms* is on top of the adjacent stack. He picks it up, turns to the first page and reads.

He has long since committed the opening sentence to memory—"In the late summer of that year we lived in a house in a village that looked across the river and the plain to the mountain"—but only gets halfway through rereading it (How many times is it now? He's lost track.) before he looks up from the book to think about the disconcerting events of the last two days. He would rather read than rerun those events. He returns to "…a village that looked across the river and the plain to the mountain." Yes, that's writing for you, he always thinks to himself when he reads Hemingway and all the other authors to whom he's attempted not to compare his own three novels—and failed at the attempt.

But he cannot concentrate on Hemingway. He wanders again to

what's going on around him, to what he is in the middle of. Through no fault of his own, he thinks. Then he thinks perhaps he ought to give some thought to revising that assumption. What of it might be his fault? Is his fault? How much of it?

Reckoning with those questions to himself, he falls asleep.

XX.

He awakens to the scent of cooking. Whatever is for breakfast is in the air, has risen to the top floor. Is Ethan actually cooking, or has Emily relented? He suspects the latter. He rouses himself. Without changing the clothes in which he slept, he goes downstairs to the kitchen. As he pads in socks, no shoes, by the second-floor back bedroom, he sees the door is closed. He sees no reason to knock. If Emily is inside, she might still be sleeping. The door to Ethan's room is open. He looks in. It appears untidy as it has all too often appeared the last few months. All evidence of anything more dramatic is absent.

When he gets to the kitchen, he stops. No Emily. It's Ethan at the oven, his back to Elihu. He's hunched over a skillet. Elihu thinks of Ethan huddling on a football field. Ethan has taken a few spices from the shelf and set them on the counter. He's sprinkling something over the skillet.

Elihu thinks it best to announce himself so the boy won't feel he's been watched. He says with, he hopes, cheer in his voice, "Good morning, Ethan."

Ethan turns around, a spice tin in one hand, a spatula in the other. He looks embarrassed. He says, "I didn't mean to surprise you. It's all right, isn't it?" He gestures towards the stove with the spatula. "Taking liberties. I already made bacon." He points to a plate piled with strips. That's what Elihu had detected from three floors above.

Elihu is tempted to say, "This is your house. Go ahead." He doesn't. He's not ready for that yet. If ever. Instead, he says, "I'm fine with it. Everything smells good. I'll just sit down and wait." He crosses the kitchen into which the morning sun is flowing from the below-stairs half windows. He pulls out a seat at the kitchen table facing Ethan and asks, "Did you find everything you need?"

Ethan says, "I've watched you long enough to see just about where everything is. I was looking for a whisk and couldn't find one, but it's okay."

"I don't think I have a whisk. I've never gotten into whisking." Saying this, Elihu hears an off-hand remark of the sort he doesn't remember exchanging with Ethan. He's taking in the tenor of this commonplace conversation. It's not that he has swapped no comments like these with Ethan over the past months, but there's a change. What is it? It's that their talk is being carried on without a layer of Ethan's predominantly low-grade uncertainty. Elihu had not articulated the trait, but it comes to him now. Simultaneously, he notices that he, too, is speaking differently. Perhaps uncertainty has informed his conversational tones as well.

It could be said, he thinks, that what Ethan and he are doing now is chatting. Chatting? *Chatting?* He's convinced that they have never simply chatted before. He's always disdained chatting. He's always found the very words "chat," "chatting" negligible. It's nothing more than small talk.

But now, so what? He's ready to continue, but attempting to see what chat he can extend past his remark about whisking, he hears Emily behind him.

She has come into the kitchen. He does not know when. He's had his back to the door. Had she been there long enough to hear the whisk talk? If so, what might she be making of it? She might assume it's been their habitual way with each other. He is not about to ask her.

Adjusting the angle on the chair a bit, he turns around and says, "Good morning."

Emily is saying, "Hello, you two. It smells awfully good in here. I could smell it all the way upstairs."

She approaches the table and pulls out one of the other three chairs, a folding chair. Elihu has never worried about matching chairs. He has stopped in far too many places for short periods of time to make matching kitchen furniture even a low priority.

Emily speaks to Ethan. "You're making omelets. You know how much I like them. You had enough eggs?"

"Elihu always has enough of most things. Or else we go out to eat."

"So for all your suffering you've been well fed," Emily says.

"That's not funny, Mom," Ethan says. "I thought you said this was no time for joking. You're right. It isn't."

"I wasn't joking. If you took it that way, I apologize."

Elihu remains quiet for this, but again he's heard the Emily he knew. How canny she can be. He knows she was joking in hopes that Ethan would see he has to fess up to something positive about his current residence. He thinks Ethan also knows his mother and knows she's right about the care he's been getting, if only as a boarder.

Ethan doesn't criticize or correct her. Instead he does something Elihu thinks he has to give the boy credit for. Ethan says, "Elihu, Emily, breakfast is ready."

They eat breakfast with Elihu remarking how good it is and how he wished he'd known this about Ethan. Not wanting to pour on the compliments too heavily to avoid sounding insincere, sounding unctuous, he says that the breakfasts he's made don't look so good in comparison. Emily says she knew Elihu would be surprised, that Ethan has been cooking since he was seven or eight. Ethan says it isn't any big thing. He likes cooking, maybe because it's easy, anyone can do it. Elihu and Emily both say it's only easy if you know how. Elihu adds that this is true of many things in life. Ethan says that aside from cooking he's never found anything that's been easy for him. "Well, reading, too." Emily asks what about getting high grades all through school? Ethan says that sure, he got high grades because everything in school was *too* easy—he had to laugh at how easy it was. He says that once when he got a good grade in Latin after doing what he estimated was minimal work, he laughed in the teacher's face. The teacher had no idea why he was laughing.

Elihu doesn't respond to this admission, but he thinks of something similar that Seth Levy does in *Wandering Youth*. The passage is based on an incident from his own high school days. He did change it significantly when writing the book. He thought he had better give it a spin, because it was a section he had written when an undergraduate and thought that Professor Penn Warren, as a teacher, might find objectionable in regard to teachers anywhere and everywhere.

That's when Elihu has a totally unexpected thought. It bothers him in one way and doesn't in another. The thought: Like father, like son.

He doesn't hang on to it. He lets it drop by offering another piece of measured praise for the omelets. He asks what spice Ethan added to them. He doesn't recognize it, he says. He hasn't identified the spice bottles on the counter. "Nutmeg," Ethan says. Elihu says that's what he thought it might be but wasn't sure.

Among the three of them the conversation goes on like that for fifteen or so minutes. When they finish, Ethan volunteers to clean up. This is also a first. Perhaps Ethan does so because he isn't going to wait for Emily to tell him to do it. Or—more likely?—he may want to give the impression he often takes on the task.

Nothing beyond thanks is said. What's said next comes from Ethan. "I'm okay in here," he says. "You two don't have to stay to watch me."

Elihu tacitly takes that as less than a polite dismissal when Ethan adds that he "can be trusted to be alone in a room where knives are handy." The remark is provocative, Elihu thinks and imagines Emily does, too, but neither Emily nor he rise to it outright. With no more than the briefest pause and an exchanged glance of agreement, they leave the room.

Emily precedes Elihu. They walk upstairs to the front parlor. She goes to the wing chair in which she sat the night before. He again sits on the burgundy couch, thinking that perhaps it was natural for her to return to the parlor but that he might have suggested they continue upstairs. Not to a bedroom, of course, but to the third floor. Then it occurs to him that remaining where they are, they can hear at least some of what is going on in the kitchen. Even if they hear nothing, should the silence begin to sound ominous, they can quickly go down the single flight of steps to reconnoiter.

Elihu notices they're both sitting at the edges of their seats and wonders whether their alert positions are dictated only by their vigilance in regard to Ethan or whether it has to do with their attitudes towards each other. This is the first time, he realizes, that they've been alone with each other for over twenty years. How remarkable, how unexpected, how... the word or words to finish the thought elude him.

He doesn't need to finish the thought. Emily says, "Do you think he's okay?"

"I hope so," Elihu says. "I don't know. I hope so. I don't want to hover over him. I don't think you do, either. That wouldn't be much of a help."

"You're right," Emily says. "It would be self-defeating, but I can't get a read on him." She pauses. "I know, I know. I'm his mother. I should know him. I do know him. Maybe I know him better than anyone. But how much do you ever know about anyone, even a son? Particularly a son. I haven't done notably well this week, have I?"

Elihu understands she's asked a rhetorical question, more to herself than to him. He doesn't respond.

She goes on. "You've been with him the last five months. You've seen him closer than I have. What's he been like? Did you see any signs of this coming? To be truthful, I don't know how you could have missed any signs."

The room is so quiet. The only sounds are faint, the running water in the kitchen, the dishwasher's hum and, from outside, neighborhood children playing on a Saturday morning.

Elihu thinks what to say. He ventures, "I'm not certain I know how to read the signs. He's kept to himself. In his room. Some days he goes out to explore the city. He told you that. When he returns, he sometimes says where he's been, what he's seen. In some way he's been…I don't know…a typical tourist. I didn't make anything special of it."

"You don't press him?" Emily asks.

"That would be like a typical nosy parent," Elihu says. "Kind of a nuisance. Many nights we go out to eat. Most nights. He doesn't say much. I've just taken that as who he was. Who he is."

Emily nods with a hint of resignation. "That's true. That is who he's been the last year or more. He wasn't at all like that when he was a child. He was talkative. He was active. I sent you the photographs. You could see it. He had friends. He changed when he was at Yale. He told us that, didn't he?"

"If you saw that happen," Elihu says, "why did you allow him to leave home?" Elihu sees Emily react to the question, looking as if she is about to speak. She doesn't. He continues. "You didn't know where he was going. What he might do, for God's sake."

Now Emily responds. "I did have a good idea where he was going." She points at the floor with her delicate right index finger. "Right here. Ethan didn't say explicitly, but it couldn't have been clearer. He dropped enough hints. In the past few months, he'd asked more questions about you than he ever had. Not constantly, but often enough for me to notice the mounting interest."

"But you couldn't be certain."

"No, but I could be fairly certain when he showed up in front of me the morning in January in his parka and with the packed bag and said he had to go off on his own. 'I need to be on my own for a while, so don't try to stop me,' he said. Or something like that. I knew enough not to try and stop him. I could have asked him if he had any idea where he was headed. I could have asked him point-blank if he was headed here, but I was just as certain he wouldn't have admitted to it. So I just said it was okay. I said to do me a favor and let me know where he was and how he was. I gave him some money and said he should let me know if he needed more. He said he would, and when he got to the front door, just before he closed it, he said, 'I thought you'd try to stop me.' I said, 'Do you want me to?' He said, 'No, I just thought you would' and closed the door behind him."

Emily pauses again. "I'm listening to myself. I sound extremely cavalier about the whole thing. I can assure you I wasn't. I'm not. There was that detective." Elihu sees her becoming more emotional—more maternal?—than she had yet been. He suppresses what is becoming a familiar urge, the urge to reach out for her. He felt, just as instinctively, that it was not the right time for that. If ever there would be a right time. "But something told me I had to do this. Ethan had to do this. You see, Elihu, for some time I'd come to the conclusion that when we were together and I got pregnant, I believed I was ready to be a mother. What I didn't bother to think about was a child's need for a father. It was a mistake, but I was only twenty-two. At that age you think you know everything, and you make mistakes."

There's an unanticipated confession, Elihu thinks, but decides not to comment on it. Emily is obviously contrite and doesn't need any rubbing in, even of the comprehending variety. He says, "But didn't you worry about him? You must have worried. A boy—Ethan—going who knows where."

Emily thinks it over. A wry smile comes to her. "When you knew me, Eli—." Ethan notes the use of "Eli." "—did you think of me as a worrier?" She doesn't wait for Elihu to answer the question. "You knew I never worried. If there was a worrier between us, it was you."

"What?" Elihu says before he can stop himself. "Why do you say that? I never worried. What did I have to worry about? I had met you—." He sees her on the Cobb Hall steps, scrabbling with her books, sees himself helping her retrieve them, her hair falling over her face, the embarrassed half-laughs that go along with that kind of awkward recovery. "—and we had our—." What adjective suffices? "Meaningful"? That isn't too gushing, is it? "—our meaningful time together. Why would I have been worrying?"

"I never said anything," Emily replies, looking him in the eyes, "but during those months, you frequently had something on your mind, something obviously preoccupying you. I remember Joyce even asked about it. 'What's he bothered about?' she once said to me. I had never noticed it. I mean I should say I never articulated it to myself, but Joyce was right. I took it as part of you. I'd have no way to trace it to any cause. I knew if I brought it up, you'd just slough it off. You'd say it was nothing. As you just did. You'd say your mind had wandered for the moment. You'd smile that smile of yours, the one you always had handy to charm the passerby of the moment. For those five months I was the one passing by most of the time."

Of all things, charm? According to her, he had charm? According to him, he didn't. He's always thought of charm as the thinnest of attributes. Elihu never thought about himself as having a smile handy to charm the random passerby. Now he knew she was right. He needed to accept he had purposely honed it in his famous-for-fifteen-asinine-minutes days. He thinks less of himself for not only working on it but for actually employing it.

Emily must be right about the worrying, too. Maybe it hadn't been worry exactly, but something related to it. Something distracting him. If he's honest, he has to admit that his mind is often other than fully committed to the immediate transaction. But isn't that true of anyone, everyone? Isn't it human that no matter how anyone is concentrated on one thing, there's always—okay, *almost* always—something else occurring to him or her? It comes as news to him that his appearance as a worrier was—is?—sufficiently more pronounced in him than in others, that others notice it in him. He knows intuitively he must concede that Emily, as well as Joyce and who knows how many others with whom he's spent any time over the years (not that many, actually—Ethan?), have watched him withdraw from conversations but have chosen to say nothing, have thought that's who he is, that's who Elihu is. He's someone who spends a lot of time somewhere else.

In the momentary silence he's allowing—and Emily is as well—Elihu thinks she must know me better than it ever occurred to me she might have. He tries to recall whenever he's been with others who suddenly acquired similar expressions that could be interpreted as their understanding he's left them for the moment. Nothing comes to him, but that could be because the giveaway expressions were there to be seen, but he hadn't seen them, he hadn't taken them in. His mind was elsewhere.

Emily—leaning towards him, her forearms resting on her lap, her hands folded—is smiling at him, a smile he takes to mean a couple things. She wants to indicate she isn't intending harsh criticism and that she also understands he's mulling what she's said and that he can take as much time as he needs. His mind is elsewhere. She has seen it before.

He decides to take further advantage of the time offered to explore, if only briefly, his typical thought processes. First thing, he thinks, is that the daily duties at which he spends most of his time do not require concentration. Shaving, washing dishes, shopping, locking doors, unlocking them, those sorts of undertakings, don't need uninterrupted concentration. Listening to music? There are times—at concerts, to which he never ventures—yes, that's where you'd be inclined to dismiss all other considerations than the sound. There are, of course, other times when music is merely welcome, but undifferentiated, background. You get lost in it but find yourself elsewhere.

That's what, for recent instance, Handel's *Concerti Grossi* were to him until a few days earlier, background music. Weren't they? Perhaps they weren't. He remembers why he turned to them. He hadn't offhandedly designated them to serve as background music to soothe the savage breast. He'd chosen them as background to soothe the agitated mind. He'd chosen them to divert his mind from—what had it been?—something disturbing about himself. Something frighteningly existential. Something that was killing him. Figuratively, of course, but almost as lethal. His mind had wandered in a dark direction, as he supposed it had more frequently than he'd want to own.

To distract himself, he has needed music, something classic, broadly imperial. He remembers now, he'd chosen music he'd first heard—music he had only recalled hearing—with Emily. How interesting. How—significant? Had, he wondered, she taken him to a concert with the express purpose of sitting him somewhere he would feel obliged to absorb the music only? Perhaps she had. On the other hand, doesn't music have the potential to conjure images? The *Concerti Grossi* have not had that effect on him. But composers—some of them, certainly—had that as their plan. So the mind straying to images of the turbulent sea, of whispering forests, of the city's bustle—of whatever—is simply music fulfilling its purpose. To dictate, not to be distracted from.

Elihu has this skein of thoughts more quickly than it seemed to him and realizes as much when Emily shifts her position and rubs her brow with the flat of her palm. "But tell me," she is saying, "didn't you pick up any signs, any signals from Ethan? Not anything? Nothing? I know you no longer think of yourself as a novelist, but surely you must retain some of the novelist's observational talents."

Elihu thinks of signs he might have seen and in time accumulated. What about Ethan's spending more and more hours behind his bedroom door? What about that night when he interrupted Elihu's reading to say he couldn't sleep? What about Ethan's more than forbidding, foreboding response to the 9/11 Memorial, his night of abusive drinking?

He says, "Maybe I should have. Maybe the night he came home drunk. Maybe I did but didn't pay sufficient attention to them."

"You said he was not that drunk."

"No, but…" How inept he feels. He did pay enough attention to speak to Ethan when it was almost too late—or seemed for those first tense minutes to be almost too late. "I don't know what gets into discontented young men. How could I?"

Emily's back straightens. She sits up. "How could you? You were a young man once. You wrote two novels about discontented young men. I'd say you know more than the average middle-aged man."

Elihu has no idea what to say to that. Emily says nothing more. To his inarguable estimation, she's made the ultimate remark. She brushes her grey trousers with her right hand while waiting for him to come up with some defense.

Just then Ethan comes into the room. He's wiping his hands with a dish towel. He says, "You two are quiet. I figured you'd be talking about me non-stop. Maybe you were. You heard me coming and stopped."

Elihu thinks that Emily's trousers straightening may have also been a signal to him that Ethan was on his way. She may have heard his footsteps on the stairs. She'd know the sound of them.

"We were discussing you," Emily says before Elihu has a chance to say anything. Not that he had anything ready to say. "And we'd come to the conclusion that we've said enough about the…the situation for now." She addresses Elihu. "Isn't that what we'd just said, Eli?"

Feeling that somehow the proceedings have been turned over to Emily, Elihu answers, putting, he hopes, some authority in his voice, "Yes, Ethan, we have said all we need to say." He hears himself sounding like a stern father to Emily's gracious mother.

Emily says, "Have you finished in the kitchen?"

"Yes," Ethan answers, and, deferentially, "everything's been put away. In the right places, I'm pretty sure."

Talk doesn't return to Ethan's suicide attempt, not to how sincere, how serious, how perhaps tepid it was meant.

The talk is of more calculated things, normal things. The talk begins a shared three-day idyll, or what could have looked to the casual observer as an idyll—could have looked like an idyll to someone unable to discern the undercurrents.

Neither Elihu nor Ethan have obligations. Over the weeks and few months they'd spent with each other, they have more or less become accustomed to their routineless routines. As for the incident, however, Elihu is aware of misgivings he needs to weigh before speaking. He knows Ethan is aware he is being watched. He knows the still required open bedroom door is the most obvious example of surveillance.

Emily doesn't have unlimited time. Sooner rather than later, Elihu assumes, she will return to Cleveland, to her marriage, though there is only the random reference to Mitchell. She offers little or nothing, really, about her work. There has been little time to focus on her. Nor is Elihu inclined to ask.

In the months Ethan has been on the impractically temperate premises, he has said next to nothing about his stepfather. The current stepfather. Mitchell. He's said even less of his previous stepfather. Elihu hasn't pressed him. He isn't that interested—or is he feigning disinterest? He allows, to himself, that he might be. Maybe he ought to be interested in the extent to which either man has influenced Ethan one way or another. Until Emily's arrival, whenever he has thought about Emily, he sees her only as she was during the University of Chicago months. The Emily with whom he's spending limited and charged time now is a new person who married her first husband only some years after he knew her. A lawyer? Then the divorce, the second marriage. To Mitchell Lombardo. The messes some people can make of their lives. Has Emily? They're the stuff of novels, of course. He's no longer a novelist.

As to Emily's work, evidently, she teaches literature, apparently, at— is it Cleveland State University? He isn't certain. He's been to Cleveland. (Taking into consideration all the drifting he's done over the decades, where hasn't he spent time?) He can picture the Euclid Avenue campus. Teaching literature is what he might have predicted for Emily. Is it American literature? Does she include on her syllabus *Wandering Youth* or *For My Betters* or both? The thought hits him drolly and suspiciously. Is it a question he's willing to ask? Any answer she might give would likely dissatisfy him in one way or other. Over the years he's wondered whether his books have been included in syllabi. The now late Saul Bellow did. Since both *Wandering Youth* and *For My Betters* continue to sell a consistent, if small-ish, amount every year, he's conjectured that literature courses might account for some percentage of the sales. Were his novels taught by Emily? That would hit too close to home for Elihu. He remembers her saying she liked them. Did she really? Or just say so, because she felt that's what he wanted to hear. Not that she ever said anything to him because she thought that's nothing other than what he wanted to hear. Maybe with his novels, she made an exception to the rule of devout honesty, a rule that was part of what he'd admired about her back then—admired, not loved, he notices himself thinking.

Because Cleveland calls her, despite her undoubtedly being on summer hiatus, but also due to the abating Ethan emergency, Emily did say she will only stay a few days. Yes, Elihu had surmised as much at seeing the small valise. Without saying so—most likely because it goes without saying—she wants to remain until she's relatively assured that the crisis is if not completely, then sufficiently, over. Not wanting to accept Ethan's word for reasons patently clear, she wants to observe his behavior for herself. She's his mother, and lets it be known in her tactful manner—a genuine gift Elihu recognizes from their happy past—that she has assessed Ethan in ways Elihu could not possibly know the boy, the young man.

They both know that much.

So a tacit pact is forged that Elihu, Ethan and Emily will perform as a family unit for a few days—not *exactly* as, it's implicitly understood, a family unit, but something along those lines.

This is new to Elihu, and he cannot, for the life of him, gauge how he feels about it. By explicit choice, he's never been a family man and doesn't know if he has the skills for it, whatever those skills are. He's witnessed families. He grew up in one with acceptable success—but not from this angle, not from this taxing perspective. He's written about families well enough to convince readers he knew what he was talking about. But so much of that was his own experience augmented by, apparently, commendable guesswork. Furthermore, he intuits that Emily has the same doubts about him but will do her best to guide him along.

Ethan understands that he has to comply fully, or else. Neither Elihu nor Emily have defined the "or else" and may not have thought it through. But it hangs in the fraught air.

"We're doing all this together," Ethan says when they're setting out for an escapade a day or two later, "because it's how you can keep an eye on me. So I don't go off to the George Washington Bridge on my own to jump off. Or to the top of the Empire State Building."

"Not funny," Emily says.

"We're doing it this way," Elihu says, "because your mother hasn't been here in a long time, and it's fun to do it together." Elihu is aware he deliberately said "fun." Hmm.

They all know the group projects are organized precisely so that Elihu and Emily *can* watch Ethan, *can* keep him occupied, can keep him not distracted so much as jollied along until he gets his own momentum going.

"Okay," Emily says, "yes, it's a way to keep an eye on you, not to let you out of our sight until we're convinced we don't have to be your vigilantes. Can you think of a good reason why we shouldn't?"

They're at the corner of East Ninth Street and Fifth Avenue, waiting for the light to change. There is no traffic. They could cross, but Emily stands her ground, as if she were with two four-year-olds whom she was teaching proper street-crossing procedure: You don't cross the street against the light, you don't make attempts to take your life, no matter how rash they are.

"Considering the current—recent—circumstances, what would you do in our shoes?" Emily says and gives Ethan a direct gaze. Elihu sees her blue eyes. He recognizes the determined glance and is once again impressed by it.

Ethan looks as if he is about to say something, then looks as if he thinks better of it. He knows Emily is right. He knows he needs to be watched. It's only fair of them to watch him, watch over him. If Elihu has it right, Ethan's is a look of concession.

It occurs to Elihu that he's often heard parents say about children—and others say about parents and their children—that children want to be disciplined. Other than a cursory nod, he never expounds on the subject. He doesn't know. He's never had children. No, make that: he has a child, a son, but he has never had anything to do with the boy's childhood. He was glad not to. If he's honest with himself, he was glad to be well out of it.

Until, that is, now.

Emily must have decided she'd made her necessary point, because, as the light changes and they head to the other side of the street, she says, "But it's true. It's not just to keep you under surveillance but also because, as Eli says, I'm glad to be doing some of the New York things I've never done. How often do I get to come here? I wish I were doing them under better circumstances. But enough of that. I'm expecting the circumstances will have improved by the time I leave. They already are improving."

She gives Ethan another of her determined glances and aims it Elihu's way as well. How remarkable it is. In it Elihu sees the Emily he knows today—is getting to know—and the Emily he knew then. It's as if the memory that had been frozen in time is thawing.

Something stirs in him he had not felt in some time. It is so vague that it takes him not only by great surprise but a fraction of a second to class: the impulse to write. To write what, he has no hint. That impulse is immediately followed by a more familiar impulse: the impulse not to write. Then a subsequent impulse: not to suppress the second impulse so quickly. Or the first one?

All this in a matter of seconds, seconds during which he realizes he's returning Emily's gaze with something approaching—what? Agreement? Conspiracy? Admiration? Feeling? He has no inclination to pin a name to it. It isn't love.

He knows it isn't love. It is not a reawakening of the feelings he had for her twenty years earlier. It's something related perhaps but different. He could put words to it. It's kind regard, the kind regard of an older man for a younger woman. Is that what he had years earlier? Hardly. Then, kind regard would have been patronizing. Still, he had not told her then that he loved her. Not in the intimate, the lucid moments. On the other hand, he must have said something in that ballpark. He still cannot get a handle on it. Then again, he is the kind of man who sometimes does tell people what they want to hear—or what he thinks they want to hear. Just, please God, to end awkward conversations.

He's done so for so long he has never questioned the need. Not the conviction that telling people what they want to hear is the easiest maneuver. It satisfies them, mollifies them. It has the capacity to end moments that might otherwise become uncomfortable, tense, even ugly. It's undoubtedly why he's made such a mission of avoiding contact. If you don't talk to people, it follows by gorgeous logic that you do not have to tell them what you think they want to hear.

Nevertheless, where Emily comes in now, something within him is—okay, not aroused, but roused.

xxi.

That explains why on the fourth or fifth night Emily is at the house—after they've returned from the Frick Museum, a midtown dinner and a movie that they all thought they would like but didn't, Elihu, still dressed, finds himself outside Emily's bedroom door, not certain why he's there, not certain why he's poised to knock but not knocking.

His curled hand is raised and has been for close to a minute when the door opens. Emily is wearing plaid pajamas and smells freshly showered. He recalls that when they were lovers—without being in love, or was she? Or was he without wanting to admit it to her or to himself?—they slept without clothes. "I heard your steps," Emily says, "and then I heard you stop. Funny how I still recognize your footsteps. Do you want to come in?"

Elihu does and doesn't. Again he's reminded of Emily's prescience, the prescience she had when she was twenty-two and plainly still has.

"Not for anything other than talking," Emily adds and has the good grace to smile. "I hope I'm not being presumptuous."

"Talk is all I had in mind," Elihu responds, without being certain that that is all he had in mind. He doesn't know what he had in mind. He doesn't know if he had anything in mind. He knows what he definitely didn't have in mind is what many would consider the obvious.

He walks into the bedroom he's occupied on impulse many nights. He knows the feel of the mattress. He knows he hasn't replaced the framed photograph of Bart and him. Nothing to worry about in that regard. He has infrequently sat in either of the two wing chairs upholstered in royal-blue broadcloth that he bought for the room. What he doesn't know about the room but recognizes is the faint aroma of cologne. It's the cologne Emily wore then. It's the cologne she still uses. He never knew what it was. He never asked the name—not from lack of interest but because he thought then that she might want to keep her choice a secret. Perhaps he was more of a romantic than he ever wants to own up to being.

He doesn't comment on it.

He just sits in one of the blue chairs.

Emily sits in the other.

"Well?" Emily says. Another smile insinuates itself. "You want to talk."

"I suppose I do," Elihu says.

"About?" Emily says that not with a demanding inflection but also not exactly with solicitation, a more congenially neutral manner. Her tone fills him with recollections. Again Mrs. Brady comes back to him. He remembers them—Emily and him—in Mrs. Brady's capacious second-floor apartment bed. He remembers them making love, the fun of it, the thrill of it, the ease of it, the passion that overtook him, the feel of Emily's body.

He wants it now. He knows he isn't going to get it. That was that Emily. This Emily is a married woman, a fortyish English teacher. He looks at this Emily and admits to himself that she's desirable but off-limits. Even though she's the mother of his—of his son—she is off-limits.

"What do I want to talk about? About Ethan," he says, assuming that's as good a place to start. It's the only place to start. It's safe ground. It's the only common ground they have to stand on. He hasn't come to the room to talk about the weather, has he?

"What about Ethan?" Emily asks, still neutral.

"What do you think?" Elihu replies.

"No," Emily comes back, "I want to know what you think. You're his father. He's your son. What do you think?"

"But you've spent so much more time with him than I have. You know him."

"He's spent the last four or five months with you. That's given you time to get to know him. You're a writer. Or *were* a writer, taking into account how you think of yourself now. And, as far as I know, have thought of yourself that way for what's going on half your life." Emily says none of this accusatorily. She's stating the facts—the fact—of his life since he stopped writing. "But I still can't imagine you've stifled your author's powers of observation. "What do you think of your son? I'll put it another way. As a writer, what do you think of Ethan as you see him now?"

"You're asking me to think as an author," Elihu says.

"I'm not asking you to resume your life as an author," Emily says. "I'm only asking you to think like one, like an author assessing a character you've created. Let's say, like a character to whom you've given birth. Like Seth Levy or Sabe Levensohn. You tell me, and then I'll tell you what I think."

She stops. She waits. She relaxes against the back of the chair, looking like a woman Elihu is glad he knows. Knows again. She asks a fair question. He thinks about it.

If he were writing Ethan, what would he see? What does he see? He begins slowly. "I see a young man who's lost his way. That's a cliché, but if I were writing it, rather than saying it, I would, of course, write it more expansively. He—Ethan—is so unsure of why he's here and where he's going that he's been foolish enough, thoughtless enough to...to...to do what he did. Why can't I say it? To try to take his life." Elihu is gathering momentum. "To indulge another cliché, his attempt, as I see it, as—. He stops himself and gives out a snide "hmm." Then, "A gesture amounting more than anything else to a call for help, as you pointed out. And he's gotten the call-back from his mother."

"*And* his father," Emily inserts.

"And his father. As you have also pointed out. Now, thanks to you—okay, to us—he's reached a point where he's taking small steps to improve. I'd like to see him taking bigger steps, strides even. Going back to school, for instance. To Yale, yes, I'd like that, and I think he would, too. But community college, if that's where he needs to start. Sorry to say, though, that as an author I can't confer even that forward step on him yet. It's too soon for me as an author to know."

"As Ethan's mother, I think you've got it right, more or less," Emily says. "I know him well enough to know he's accomplished what he set out to do when he swallowed those pills. Whether he knew consciously that's what he intended, he's provided himself with what he's never had. A mother and a father. The sly…" She lets the sentence trail off.

Elihu takes in her assessment. Whose powers of observation are stronger now, he wonders. He's inclined to say Emily's. Ethan's manipulating the outcome she sees has escaped him. Perhaps because he was too close, too involved to maintain the author's perspective he might have maintained in different circumstances. He hadn't noticed before, but can this be some sign of—to put a conventional spin on it—a father-son thing? The father in this case being him? Him? Free agent Elihu Goulding?

"You've got a better writer's take on this than I have. Maybe *you* could write it," Elihu says.

Emily laughs. She hasn't laughed often during the visit. Smiled from time to time but not laughed. Elihu hears it now and also hears it from long ago. It has the sound of a descending scale played on fine crystal goblets. "No," she says, "I'm not the writer. You are. You still are, and here, right in front of you is autobiography to fictionalize. Just as you did your own youth."

She gives him another of the acute stares she's refined over the years.

"No, no," Elihu says. "If I fictionalized this—not that I ever would or would ever even begin to—I'd have to work in at least one more suicide attempt. At the very least. Or a breakout. Or a break*down*. I don't want that for Ethan. I couldn't write that. It would feel ridiculously contrived."

"See," Emily says. "You do still think like a novelist."

"Only because you railroaded me into it."

"Then here's my chance at a cliché. You can lead a horse to water, but you can't make him drink."

"Sorry to say you haven't gotten me anywhere near water. That died with *Wandering Youth* and *For My Betters* and was buried six feet under with *The Accidental Immigrants*."

At that, Emily momentarily presses her lips together. It's the look of discovery, of confirmation, of pleased one-upmanship. "You got that right. Something was buried with *The Accidental Immigrants*. You had a book that in your estimation fell short of your first two phenomena. That happens to any number of writers, but they don't give up. You did. You put all your books out of sight, out of mind. As near as I can figure, you worked hard at sublimating them, smothering them even."

This line of thought, Elihu realizes, is disturbing him. He's moved to say something.

Emily anticipates him. "No, you had your say," she says raising her speaking level a notch. "I said I'd tell you what I think after you spoke. I'm doing that. Evidently, you sublimated your books extremely effectively in all the years you've lived here and there and who knows where. Do you even remember all the places you temporarily passed through? *Wandering*

Youth, indeed. That was self-inflicted prophecy. Wandering middle-aged man. You've done such a thorough job of discarding the past that you've forgotten sentences, paragraphs, pages, entire chapters of what goes on in those first-rate novels."

Elihu wants to deny this but recognizes he cannot. Wherever he's lived, his novels are on shelves or in stacks or hidden in cabinets. But wherever they are, he doesn't reread them. Why should he, only to be reminded? Of what? Of how they might have been affected if he'd known about his mother's miscarriage? Which he might have done had he been writing his mother's story, not his? Of how good they are? Of how unsatisfying they are? Which would be worse? Why subject himself to that?

"You've pushed them so far to the back of your mind, Eli, that you've forgotten who Seth Levy is, what he does. You've forgotten that Seth Levy goes through a period when he's depressed and thinks about taking his life. You've completely forgotten you devote half of a *Wandering Youth* chapter to Seth Levy testing ropes, determined to settle on the one that's absolutely too strong to break in a hanging."

She's right, Elihu thinks. She remembers his novels better than he does. She has to be teaching them or must have taught them at some time. Now the chapter to which she's referring comes back to him. He says, "But Seth Levy—."

Emily interrupts him. "You're going to say he doesn't go through with it. Doesn't matter. He thinks about it. You know that Ethan has read all your novels, don't you? Maybe he didn't tell you. He didn't tell me at first. I think he would read them when I was out of the house. He'd put them back in the bookcase exactly where he found them so I wouldn't notice. He only admitted it recently. While he was thinking about a trip here, I daresay. You might even say, if you wanted to, that you and Seth Levy put the idea of suicide in his head."

"Just a min—," Elihu starts to say something brusque, his dander now way up.

Again Emily stops him. "You're angry. Look at it this way. If you didn't think it was possible, you'd laugh it off. You're not laughing. I'm not saying Ethan read *Wandering Youth* and immediately set a plan in motion. But, and you know this, readers are impressionable. They must be. They have to be. Otherwise, why would anyone write?"

"So what you're saying is," Elihu says with enough force that he sees Emily choosing to hear him out, "I'm responsible for Ethan's stupid… whatever."

"No, but yes," Emily says. "And as far as that goes, you've only heard the beginning of what I want to say. It's not Seth Levy alone who put the suicide idea in his head and kept it there. Not by a long shot. You did. Elihu Goulding."

Elihu is impelled to say something to that.

Emily anticipates him again. "Let me speak. Ethan isn't the only reason I'm here. I've been wanting to say this to you for a long time. Many times it crossed my mind to say it in Chicago, but I was young then. I thought I could be wrong. What did I know? I was just a University of Chicago undergraduate, and you were Elihu Goulding. You were *the* Elihu Goulding.

"I decided it wasn't my place to say it then, but I'm saying it now. Maybe it's not my place. I still wonder about that, but who else would say it to you? You've allowed no one close enough to. When Ethan did what he did, he wasn't imitating Seth Levy. He was taking after you. How? Why? Because you also committed suicide. You know you did. Like father, like son. The irony of it."

Like father, like son, Elihu hears it again.

"You killed off Elihu Goulding, the novelist," Emily, leaning towards him, insists. "The novelist Elihu Goulding killed off that part of himself. He did the bold character in when he was less than fifteen years older than Ethan is now. It was as decisive a suicide as there ever was."

Elihu opens his mouth to speak but has no idea what he wants to say.

"Don't try to tell me I'm wrong," Emily says.

Elihu isn't inclined just then to tell her she's wrong. Instead he hears himself thinking, "Something's killing me, and I don't know what it is." The phrase he blurted in the library-study on the first day he arrived at 73 East Ninth Street. No, he isn't thinking the terrifying, the terrified quote. He's spoken it, not loudly, more like a murmur.

"What did you say?" Emily asks.

"Nothing," Elihu says, trying to—hoping to—recover lost ground. But he knows it's not nothing. Emily has hit on something. He needs to brood on it further. Not brood, anything but brood. All right, contemplate it. Fix on it. Suicide. The nothing-to-live-for aspect of it. In those departed days did he, like Ethan, grapple with the notion that he had nothing to live for? Have all his calculatedly aimless peregrinations been an undisclosed-to-himself journey to find that something? Would he recognize it were it standing right in front of him?

Emily is waiting for more of an answer.

He says, "Just talking to myself."

What Emily said to bring on the brief rumination was how ironic it is that Ethan's action is akin to Elihu's decision to write no longer. Yes, like father, like son. Elihu considers the phrase anew. It's threatening to take on the air of a leitmotif.

That's not what he says to Emily, though. He says, "I'm sorry that's what you think about my choice."

Emily's expression doesn't change. She holds on to it to confirm that she's holding fast to what she's said. "Yes, it's what I think. I wish you did, too—face up to it."

Neither of them moves, another way they maintain their view of the fragile matter. They sit in silence for several seconds.

Then Emily speaks, giving Elihu another of the appealing curve-lipped smiles he increasingly realizes he likes, has always liked, has seen whenever he thinks of her over the years. He *has* thought of her. She does stand out, along with only a few of the women comprising his not infrequent dalliances—the last one a Bedford widow who was worth his generally valueless time. Most of them, he thought then, and continues thinking, were ways to squander the weeks, the months—pleasurably for the most part, but at the end of the day as disposable as last year's sports statistics. Perhaps to his credit, he never kidded himself that in the longer or shorter run he wasn't leading the women on—and didn't admire himself for it.

Now, while saying nothing, he concedes that he was leading himself on, too. And isn't that, he asks himself—in the stillness filled most noticeably with Emily's subtly fragrant cologne—also a form of suicide?

The silence broken by her prefatory smile, she offers, "I think we've said as much as we have to say to each other tonight. It's time we went to bed." She rises from the chair. It's almost as if she's concluding an interview with someone applying for a job, or, more appropriately, with a student discussing a final grade he considers unfair.

Elihu gets up, too, and follows Emily to the bedroom door. She opens it and waits for him to walk into the hallway. Just before she closes the door, she says, "Do me a favor, Elihu, will you? Please give some thought to what I said."

She shuts the door, making no sound.

Elihu stands in the hallway, wanting to say something, but once again doesn't know what he might say were Emily still poised to hear him.

He walks along the hallway, aware of his slow gait. As usual he isn't wearing shoes, only socks. Sometimes he wears the same pair of socks for three or four days. For Emily's sake, though not previously Ethan's, he's changed his socks every day she's been in the house.

He stops by Ethan's slightly ajar door to listen. Nothing. He walks up the stairs, undresses, gets into the convertible bed at the farther end of the room. Wondering whether he will dream and if so, wondering what the dream, or succession of dreams, might tell him, he falls asleep.

xxii.

In the morning, there is no talk of Ethan's failed suicide attempt or Elihu's unending attempt, as Emily has it. Elihu is still weighing it to himself.

The three of them go about the morning business as if they've been doing as much for some time, as if this were established family custom. Elihu offers to make breakfast, and it's agreed, with Ethan setting the table and Emily favored to make coffee.

When it's brewed and Elihu is still scrambling the eggs and frying the bacon, Emily leaves the room. At the top of the stairs she makes a cell phone call. Elihu can't hear what she's saying over the noise coming from the stove.

When she returns, she says she has just talked to Mitchell and that, although he reports he's doing fine at home, she thinks it's time she returned to him. More than that, she's left her work long enough. It's time to get back to it. There's some sort of imminent meeting at the college about the coming school year.

When she says Mitchell's name, it takes Elihu a second or two to place it. She and Ethan have mentioned it several times, of course, but Elihu sees that when it comes up, he somehow is resisting taking it in. And there have been other things on his mind.

"He's a fine man," she says to Elihu. "You'd like him. He's not a writer, but he's a reader." Then she says something that does catch Elihu off guard. "I suppose that after you, I couldn't be with anyone who doesn't at least like books. He's read your novels. He said he liked them. I didn't quiz him on them, but I'm sure he meant it. Mitchell is honest to a fault. If he hadn't liked them, he would have said so."

Perhaps consciously, Elihu has avoided working up a mental image of Mitchell. Now he imagines a fifty-ish man in casual clothes sitting in a reading chair holding a book. He says to Emily, "Does he smoke a pipe?"

The question sets Ethan off. Seated at the kitchen table waiting for his bacon and eggs, he says, "Smoke a pipe? That's a laugh. Mitchell is one of the great anti-smokers. But I gotta give it to him. He's why I don't smoke."

When Ethan says that, what Elihu hears is that Mitchell has been responsible for significant parental influence, if only on this smoking issue. Elihu has never smoked thanks to Jean and Morris. Jean eventually quit. Morris tried but didn't succeed. From guilt that all but reddened their faces, they warned him off it with the forever repeated "filthy habit" opprobrium. It took.

Elihu has a nostalgic thought about Seth Levy not being a smoker, but whereas Seth Levy could get suicide circling in Ethan's head, he evidently isn't the non-smoking role model Mitchell is. Did Ethan even notice that Seth Levy never smokes?

Is it jealousy Elihu is feeling or is he just understanding that had he been fathering Ethan these couple of decades, things would be different? He hasn't been. He doesn't know when Emily married Mitchell. He hasn't really been more than offhandedly interested. For some years now Mitchell has been Ethan's father. Specifically a stepfather, yes, but after a while in many instances in many families, doesn't the "step" part dispel? Especially if a biological parent is absent, has chosen to be absent on whatever dubious excuse?

Many stepsons take their stepfather's surname, Elihu thinks. Has

Ethan ever thought about that step? It's not a question Elihu would ever ask, even if at the moment he could remember what the name is. Lombardo. Yes, Mitchell Lombardo. Ethan might have chosen to become Ethan Lombardo. He could find out if that were ever a possibility, but not by asking Emily or Ethan. Too embarrassing. Since all checks were sent to Emily, he could ask at the lawyers' office. The checks. No, that wouldn't do. Emily hadn't taken a married name. Not either time. He knows she'd kept her name, being intent on keeping, as so many women do, the surname she was born with. Had she and he married (ha!), she never would have been Emily Goulding. And if she hadn't become Emily Lombardo, Ethan likely would never make the change.

Now figuring he should say something about the not-smoking situation, Elihu says, "Mitchell is right. You're much better off not to. If you had, I would have needed to get ashtrays in." He remembers that many years before, a reader had sent him as a thank-you for his novels, a Havana Club ashtray. Why the man assumed he smoked cigars eluded him. He certainly was never holding a cigar in any of the author photographs Jill Krementz took. He sent the man a thank-you note and put the ashtray away somewhere. Where it is is another unknown. Tossed or lost, he supposes. He imagines Ethan and him smoking cigars together, something he thinks he has seen fathers and sons do, often with fatuous smiles on their faces. That's ripe for a laugh, he thinks.

Emily says, "It's a good thing you didn't have to do that. Ashtrays. A waste of space. A nuisance to cart from one place to the next." Elihu picks up on the friendly sarcasm in the remark but doesn't think it needs a reply. Emily goes on,

"Since I'm leaving, Ethan, I'd like to know what you want to do."

Ethan has put away his breakfast with the speed to which Elihu has become familiar. He recognizes that as his own practice at Ethan's age. He doesn't remember if Seth Levy or Sabe Levensohn put away any breakfasts at breakneck speeds.

"Aren't you and Elihu going to talk to me anymore about…about what happened?" Ethan asks with one of the uncertain looks he's used over the time he's been around the house. He looks at Emily and Elihu, at Emily first.

Elihu doesn't know what he's expected to say to that. He ought to say something.

Emily knows what she wants to say and, signaling Elihu with a confident look that she'll handle this, says, "No, Ethan we're not. Your"—she takes the briefest pause before the next word—"father and I have decided you made a mistake and are now dealing with it properly, doing well with it. We think you're over it enough to make your own decisions without one of us or both of us deciding for you." She turns to Elihu. "Isn't that what we're thinking, Elihu?"

When she says this, Ethan also looks at Elihu. In his expression and in the way in which he has impulsively leaned towards Elihu, he not only reveals but, more than that, exposes a need Elihu cannot fully nail but simultaneously intuits: that the need Ethan is exposing connects with a need of his own, a need he'd never acknowledged, or even detected in himself.

"Yes, Ethan, your mother and I are agreed," Elihu says and not entirely because he is impelled to. In the way he's phrased it, he recognizes an instinctive element not necessarily new to him where Emily is concerned.

Pleased that Elihu has said what she so obviously—to him—wanted him to say, Emily again addresses Ethan. "Your life is your own, Ethan. You're old enough to understand that. You can do what you want with it. Of course, your father"—this time she doesn't pause between "your" and "father"—"and I wish you would use it well."

As if he's left his body and is observing himself from above, Elihu sees a man having no issue with the use of "father." He sees that Emily has carefully chosen how and when to invoke the word. Also as she's speaking, Elihu observes how much Emily has become the woman she is and the woman foreshadowed in the young woman he knew.

Ethan says, "I know the two of you would like me to go back to Yale, but I'm not ready for that. Not yet."

Emily starts to respond to that, but Elihu intercedes, saying, "We don't expect you to pack your bags and leave for New Haven today or tomorrow. Just to keep it in mind as a privilege you've earned and deserved and don't want to ignore without giving yourself a good reason. Just keep it in mind as an option."

Hearing himself say that, Elihu comes back to himself and catches an astonishing—to him—new tone in his voice. He's one of two allied parents advising a child out of serious concern.

Ethan listens and then says, with a bemused smile Elihu has never seen before, "Yes, Dad."

Elihu thinks how he's never heard those words aimed at him before, and he's not especially surprised he has no objection to being their target.

"I'm packed and leaving very soon," Emily says, looking at her watch. It's not the same watch she wore when Elihu knew her back then. It's a more practical watch. "I've ordered a car for about a half hour from now. If you're coming with me, Ethan, you'd better pack in a hurry. I'd be glad to have you home again, and so would Mitchell. He asked if you'd be coming with me. I said I didn't know."

She looks at Ethan expectantly. Ethan makes more of a show of thinking it over than he needs to and says, "I think for the time being I'd like to stay here with…Elihu." It's fairly obvious he was deciding how he wanted to situate Elihu for the three of them. "That's if Elihu doesn't mind."

Elihu hears himself say, and without hesitation, "I don't mind at all. Why would I?" Then he laughs. At himself—and cannot remember when he last did that.

"Then that's settled," Emily says.

"If you need me to help you, Mom," Ethan says, "I'm glad to."

Emily says, "Thanks, son, but why don't you and Elihu clean up the kitchen instead? It could use it after the first-rate breakfast."

She leaves the room to go upstairs. For the next while the only sounds in the house are domestic sounds. Elihu and Ethan clean up the kitchen, not saying much to each other but perhaps, Elihu thinks, more comfortable in each other's presence than they have been.

A honking horn gets their attention. Emily, heard coming from the bedroom floor, calls down to alert them about the car. Ethan runs up from the kitchen, asking if he can bring Emily's bag down. Though Ethan and Elihu have not completely finished in the kitchen, Elihu follows, wiping his hands on a dish towel. Emily answers that she's already seen to her bag, that there isn't that much to see to.

Elihu puts the dish towel on the small table next to the staircase. He notices Emily is wearing the same pink blazer and grey slacks she was wearing when she arrived, the same filmy scarf around her neck.

Ethan has picked up the valise she brought with her. He's opened the door and is going down the front stairs. Emily says to Elihu, "His staying is all right with you, isn't it?"

"Yes, sure," Elihu says. "I've gotten used to him. "To—," he says, meaning it to be, and not to be, a joke, "—my boy. Of course, I don't know if he's gotten used to me."

"That's up to him," Emily says, and comes over to Elihu. She reaches out to hug him. As when she arrived, he isn't ready for that again but goes along with it. When they have their arms around each other, Emily leans back to look Elihu in the eyes. She says, "You know, don't you—or how could you?—that I still love you. I always will. You've given me so much of yourself. Of that part of yourself that you were willing, or able, to give. I'm not just talking about Ethan. He's your greatest gift to me, but before that, giving me the sense of myself you gave a young girl so long ago by simply spending time with her. Considering who you were. Not who you were, but who I knew you were. That young girl will always love you."

Elihu feels he should say something, but Emily, who has so often anticipated him, says, "You don't have to say anything. I know how you feel."

"But I don't know how I feel," Elihu says.

"You do. You're just not aware of it now. You will be."

They're interrupted by Ethan shouting from the street. "The car, the car."

Elihu and Emily let go of each other with what are very much like knowing looks.

They go out and down the stoop. There are seven steps, Elihu allows himself to acknowledge. The valise is already in the trunk. The driver is closing the hood.

Emily hugs and kisses Ethan and gets into the car. The window is open by her. She faces out and says, "You two be good to each other." She tells the driver to set off.

Elihu thinks that the last time they parted she was the one setting off then, too. Ethan is standing next to him, waving. It occurs to Elihu to put his arm around Ethan's thick right shoulder. He does. He feels Ethan's arm go around his widened waist. They stand like that until the car carrying Emily disappears at the corner.

They drop their arms to go back up the seven-stairs stoop. Elihu fumbles in his pants pocket for the front-door key. He doesn't need the key. They'd left the forest-green door ajar. They close it behind them to become whatever, together and separately, they're going to become in the unforeseeable years ahead.

www.ingramcontent.com/pod-product-compliance
Lightning Source LLC
LaVergne TN
LVHW041631060526
838200LV00040B/1536